CHRIS WOMERSLEY IS the bestselling, award-winning author of four novels – *The Low Road*, *Bereft*, *Cairo* and *City of Crows* – which have been published around the world and translated into several languages. Chris's short fiction has appeared in *Granta*, *The Best Australian Stories*, *Meanjin* and *Griffith Review* and has won or been shortlisted for numerous prizes. This is his first short fiction collection. Chris lives in Melbourne with his wife and son. Contact him at: chriswomersley.com

Also by Chris Womersley

The Low Road
Bereft
Cairo
City of Crows

ACCOLADES AND AWARDS FOR CHRIS WOMERSLEY

Winner of Indie Award for Best Fiction
Winner of the ABIA Literary Fiction Book of the Year
Winner of the Ned Kelly Award for Fiction
Winner of the Josephine Ulrick Prize for Literature
Shortlisted for the Miles Franklin Literary Award
Shortlisted for the ALS Gold Medal for Literature
Shortlisted for *The Age* Book of the Year
Shortlisted for the Victorian Premiers' Award for an Unpublished Manuscript
Shortlisted for the Gold Dagger Award for International Crime Fiction

*

'One of the unrepentantly daring and original talents in the landscape of Australian fiction.'
SYDNEY MORNING HERALD

'As unflinching as Cormac McCarthy, and as perverse as Ian McEwan.'
AUSTRALIAN FINANCIAL REVIEW

'Womersley plunges readers into [a] dark, dangerous, magical and pungent world.'
AUSTRALIAN WOMEN'S WEEKLY

'By interweaving the trivial, the humorous and the grisliest of the grisly, Chris Womersley straps us in for a shivery ride.'
NEW YORK TIMES

'More straight-talking than John Banville, less tricksy than Julian Barnes, Womersley nonetheless shares his British counterparts' interest in the adult man forged in the flames of intense youthful experience.'
THE AGE

'Clear, evocative and powerful; an utter joy.'
IRISH TIMES

'Just once in a while a thriller comes along that is so good it takes your breath away. Australian journalist Womersley's second novel does that in a heartbeat . . . It's a thriller worthy of Hitchcock: taut, poignant and unexpected.'
DAILY MAIL

'A master storyteller.'
AUSTRALIAN BUSINESS REVIEW

'Chris Womersley cements his place as one of Australia's finest writers in this taut gothic suspense story.'
THE BIG ISSUE

'Poetic and original.'
THE MONTHLY

'Chris Womersley knows how to shine light into the darkest corners of rural Australia.'
MICHAEL ROBOTHAM

'Haunting and beautiful.'
SUNDAY TELEGRAPH

'A nightmare labyrinth where superstition rules and where it seems the Devil calls the tune.'
THE AUSTRALIAN

'This grim but spellbinding book is a danse macabre to the tune of Womersley's incantatory prose . . . Worth reading for the writing alone.'
KIRKUS REVIEWS

'A harrowing adventure and an enchanted exploration of the seductive worlds of faith, hope, love, lust and longing.'
THE ADVERTISER

'A merciless read, taking you by the throat and not letting go for a minute.'
AUSTRALIAN LITERARY REVIEW

'So stark and pitiless that it's hard to keep reading. But it's harder to stop.'
GIDEON HAIGH

'Chris Womersley, in plain and startling yet tender and lyrical prose, has constructed a moving narrative that opens up the wounds of war, laying bare the events that pre-date the conflict and reach forward into the collective memory . . . War is the big drama of human horror, but the basest acts of cruelty are also enacted in what passes for peacetime. That Womersley can marry these two extremes, and construct a narrative in which the reader is left with a burning sense of regret and tenderness, is a mark of his skill and of his fictional reach.'
AUSTRALIAN BOOK REVIEW

'The quiet whispering tone of this book will linger long after you've finished it.'
COURIER-MAIL

'This unabashedly gothic tale possesses such luminous beauty and emotional acuity that it has already evoked praise as lavish, if not more so, as that which greeted *The Low Road* . . . *Bereft* strikes nary a false note as it maps out the haunting, ambiguous territory between the trauma of war and grief, memory and longing, in a story of injustice and revenge that haunts long after reading.'
CANBERRA TIMES

'Somehow Chris Womersley peers deep into the suffering heart and sees beyond the pain that humans inflict on each other, to a place where dignity, loyalty and even affection might blossom. He writes with such compelling power it is barely possible to put the book down.'
DEBRA ADELAIDE

CHRIS WOMERSLEY

A LOVELY AND TERRIBLE THING

PICADOR

First published 2019 in Picador by Pan Macmillan Australia Pty Ltd
1 Market Street, Sydney, New South Wales, Australia, 2000

Copyright © Chris Womersley 2019

The moral right of the author to be identified as
the author of this work has been asserted.

All rights reserved. No part of this book may be reproduced
or transmitted by any person or entity (including Google,
Amazon or similar organisations), in any form or by any means,
electronic or mechanical, including photocopying, recording,
scanning or by any information storage and retrieval system,
without prior permission in writing from the publisher.

 A catalogue record for this book is available from the National Library of Australia

Typeset in 12.2/17 pt Adobe Garamond Pro by Post Pre-press Group

Printed by McPherson's Printing Group

This is a work of fiction. Characters, institutions and organisations
mentioned in this novel are either the product of the author's imagination
or, if real, used fictitiously without any intent to describe actual conduct.

 The paper in this book is FSC® certified. FSC® promotes environmentally responsible, socially beneficial and economically viable management of the world's forests.

For Freya

'Let the most absent-minded of men be plunged in his deepest reveries—stand that man on his legs, set his feet a-going, and he will infallibly lead you to water, if water there be in all that region . . . Yes, as everyone knows, meditation and water are wedded forever.'

Herman Melville, *Moby-Dick: or, The Whale*

CONTENTS

Headful of Bees	1
The House of Special Purpose	11
The Possibility of Water	21
The Very Edge of Things	31
Growing Pain	41
Petrichor	51
The Middle of Nowhere	71
The Other Side of Silence	87
The Mare's Nest	99
The Age of Terror	109
Dark the Water, So Deep the Night	119
Where There's Smoke	145
Season of Hope	153
A Lovely and Terrible Thing	167
Blood Brother	183
Crying Wolf	187
The Deep End	203
The Shed	227
Theories of Relativity	237
What the Darkness Said	253
Acknowledgements	267
Details of previous publication	269

Headful of Bees

IF, YEARS LATER, you heard that little Adam Miller had joined a cult, you wouldn't have been totally surprised: he had an unhinged sort of quality, that too-shiny light you see in the eyes of those Manson Family girls or Hare Krishna devotees handing out leaflets in the city. He was the kid in our street who found a pile of old *Playboy* magazines by the railway line, who would come to school with a dozen packets of bubblegum for his friends, who saw movies the rest of us weren't allowed to see yet. I envied his family in the way you envy other families when you're young. The other parents are always cooler or prettier than your own; they let you stay up later, do stuff your own parents would never allow. I thought he was lucky, although my opinion on that has, obviously, changed over time.

Adam had an unusual home situation and he and I became friends, or at least we hung out a lot after school – listening to his sister's records, sometimes kicking a football around, eating Milo straight from the tin. His house was empty most afternoons from when we got home from school until dinnertime, sometimes even later. They were dim hours, full of strange magic, of things we would never again see or feel. We were young, on the brink of adulthood, those few years when almost everything in your life really happens.

Mr Miller was a scientist. He worked at the university – long hours and late nights, that sort of thing. Mrs Miller was a nurse but she'd been away for several months, staying with relatives out of town. She was a distant woman at the best of times, sick of her children, or so it had always seemed to me. I'd heard plenty of stories about her – we all had. One night the previous winter I was putting out the rubbish bins and encountered her on the footpath in the dusk light. She was leaning against the fence, smoking a cigarette, and seemed not to notice me straightaway, so absorbed was she in her meditations.

'Hello, Mike,' she said in a soft voice as I wrestled the heavy bin to the kerb. 'And how are you this evening?'

I feigned surprise. 'Oh, hi, Mrs Miller. I'm fine, thanks. How are you?'

'Oh, you know. Taking in the night air.'

I nodded and looked around, although I was unsure what I might have been looking for exactly. The streetlights came on. My God, those suburban evenings, so full of hope and all its little victims. That smell of muddy grass, the clatter of spoon against a dog's dinner bowl, a puddle of wine on the kitchen table.

Mrs Miller tapped her forehead with the packet of Marlboros, and the cigarettes rattled about inside, the sound of them like a battery of tiny coughs. *Cough cough cough cough.* It was an unsettling gesture, made more so by her accompanying low groan.

The previous week a dog, or maybe a possum, had tipped over our bin and rummaged through the contents, so I busied myself with jamming the metal lid on tight. When I had finished, Mrs Miller was staring at me intently.

Like some sort of Cold War femme fatale, she took a lengthy drag on her cigarette and exhaled the pale smoke into the air. 'How old are you now?'

'I'm almost fourteen.'

'Nearly fourteen – wow. What an age. With everything in front of you. What are you going to do for a job when you're older?'

'I don't know, Mrs Miller. I quite like science. Maybe a biologist or something?'

She pondered this. 'Why don't you call me Vivian? You're old enough now. We're neighbours after all.'

I nodded.

'Come on. Try it out.'

I stared up the length of the street, at the wet asphalt gleaming under the streetlights like the hide of a whale. A car cruised past. 'Okay, Vivian,' I said.

'There you go.' She pushed off the fence and tottered towards me on her high heels. Since the lights had come on and my eyes had adjusted to the gloom, I saw that her skirt was askew and a leaf was lodged in her dark, tangled hair; she looked, in fact, like she had been climbing trees.

'I have bees in my head,' she hissed at last, in a conspiratorial tone that suggested such misfortune might have been the fault of someone nearby. 'Waiting to . . . come out and *take over*.'

Caught off guard and with the image of her climbing a tree still uppermost in my mind, I shrank back, as if expecting to see a swarm of the insects wriggling about in her hair.

Perhaps detecting my alarm, she hurriedly corrected herself. 'I feel like I have bees in my head, I'm supposed to say. I *feel like* I have a head full of bees, trying to crawl out. That's all. I realise there's nothing in there. I just . . . I don't know.' She flicked her cigarette butt expertly into the wide street. A sudden, unconvincing laugh. 'Run along, Mike. Say hi to your mum for me.'

That was about a year earlier and I had hardly seen her since.

Adam had become obsessed with the Van Morrison album *Astral Weeks* and would play it over and over again on the turntable in his sister's room. Sitting on the floor cross-legged, chin on his fists, weaving from side to side in time with the music. The record had been released the year he was born – 1968 – and this only added to its appeal. That, plus the indecipherable lyrics, its whiff of the mystical. I guess that's what I meant about him being the sort of kid who might have joined a cult or otherwise been seduced by some extravagant promise. He had that searching quality, always pointing out something in the music and asking what I thought old Van was wailing on about.

'There,' he'd say with a finger raised, peering at me through his grubby fringe. 'What does he *mean*? Is he riding a bike or what? And where's Ladbroke Grove, do you reckon? England, I guess.'

I shrugged. I was poking about in his sister's stuff on the bureau. Sally was four or five years older than us. She was meant to be looking after Adam in their mother's absence but we rarely saw her; she was always heading out with her plumber boyfriend, Gary, going to the drive-in, promising to take us to see *Poltergeist* even though, of course, she never did. There was a Led Zeppelin poster on her wall, pictures of David Bowie torn from magazines. In a metal dish were assorted hairclips, a collection of badges, and a bottle of pink nail polish. Clothes were strewn over the floor and the bed.

The side came to an end and I crouched down to sort through the other albums stacked against the wall. I was familiar with most of Sally's records but enjoyed looking at the covers and reading the liner notes. She had the usual stuff – some Stones, Cheap Trick, Fleetwood Mac.

'Hey,' Adam said, tossing the *Astral Weeks* cover to one side, 'guess what I found yesterday?'

He jumped up and began riffling through his sister's drawers. After a few seconds he held up his trophy: a slim joint. He wafted it beneath his nose. 'I think Gary gets hold of some pretty good stuff,' he said, affecting the tone of an expert, even though I knew he had never been stoned himself.

I took it, rolled it between my fingers and sniffed. When I'd puffed on a joint in the bathroom at the school social the previous year, I hadn't really felt anything, even though I had willed the tiles to transform, the fluorescent light to reveal something of the world's great mysteries. Nothing, except a mild headache, probably from the tobacco.

Adam snatched the joint from me. He was excited. 'What do you think? Should we smoke it?'

The very thought of it made me anxious. 'Oh, I don't know. Sally will kill us.'

'What's she going to do? Tell my dad?'

This was a good point. I made a show of checking my watch. 'I'm not sure. It's getting late. What about Gary?'

Adam rolled his eyes. 'Who cares about Gary?'

'Well, it might be his joint.'

'If he says anything, I'll tell my dad that Sally's boyfriend is a drug dealer and he'll call the cops straightaway. Come on. We'll open the window and blow the smoke outside. It'll be fine.'

I shrugged and turned back to the records, kind of hoping he would forget the idea. But he didn't. He found Sally's lighter, opened the window and perched on its ledge. Then he lit up, took a few tokes and passed it to me.

The following few hours are soggy in my memory. We watched a cat stalk a bird in the garden below. Rainwater dripped from a tree. Traffic, the distant hoot of a train, the soft glimmer of angels. There was a lot of heavy staring, of giggling at things I have long forgotten. Adam insisted on listening to the first side of *Astral Weeks* again, which suddenly sounded melancholy, riddled with portents.

I became incredibly thirsty and, leaving Adam lying on the floor, arranged my limbs to make my way through the gloomy house into the kitchen to hunt down something sweet and wet to drink. The hallway was cold. A dish on a sideboard rattled as I passed.

I was standing in the wedge of light from the open fridge door, cold juice bottle in one hand, when I noticed Mrs Miller sitting at the kitchen table. The shock of her. Like when I had seen her in the street the year before, she showed no sign of having spotted me, but it was impossible that she hadn't. Sure enough, she turned to face me after a few seconds. A cigarette burned in a glass ashtray. All was quiet.

'Hi there,' she said at last.

I was terrified, paranoid, unable to speak. Eventually, I held up the bottle of juice and mumbled something about getting a drink. Surely, I thought, surely she would know instantly that I was stoned out of my mind. She would tell my mum, ring the police, throw me out of the house.

But she just waved a hand in the air. 'Go right ahead.'

As naturally as I could, concentrating on every move, I lifted a glass from the cupboard and poured orange juice into it. Mrs Miller didn't speak but I was horribly aware of her scrutinising me. I put away the juice, closed the fridge and was preparing to flee when she spoke.

'No need to run off,' she said. 'I haven't seen you in ages. How's your mother?'

I hesitated, stranded in the no-man's-land between the kitchen door and the wooden table where she was sitting. 'She's fine,' I managed to croak.

'And your dad?'

'He's good, too.'

'What are you boys up to? Listening to Sally's records?'

I nodded.

'And where's she?'

'Out with Gary somewhere, I think.'

She inspected me. 'What did they tell you about me? What did Adam tell you?'

I shrugged. My mouth was claggy and dry. The bulge of fear in my chest was swelling right up into my throat. I wasn't sure what she was asking me, whether I had even understood her.

'Did they say I was with relatives all this time?' she asked.

'Yes,' I answered, relieved to finally understand. 'In Queensland.'

She found this inordinately funny, and giggled for a few seconds. 'Yes. They taught me to meditate. To drink herbal tea. We wrote long lists of things we were grateful for. Children, houses, our *health*, of course.'

I was desperate for Adam to appear and rescue me but, with dismay, I detected the murmuring intro to the opening track on *Astral Weeks*' second side. There was no way he would even hear us now.

'Didn't work, though,' she said. She coughed several times and patted her chest. She undid a button or two of her dark blue blouse and pinched the fabric free from her chest, as if she were hot.

I began to back away, hoping to melt into the gloomy hallway without her noticing. And I was almost at the kitchen door when she composed herself and gestured for me to approach. My skin rippled with fresh fear.

'Don't be scared,' she said. 'Come *here*.' Her tone was firm, but playful. I shuffled across and stood in front of her. I caught a thrilling glimpse down her blouse: the lacy edge of her black bra, the slope of breast beneath it. Its rapid rise and fall. A fine gold chain lounged across the ridge of her collarbone. She looked me up and down and smiled, but in a way that made her seem regretful. 'I've known you almost all your life, you know. When we first met you were a boy in short pants. I remember thinking you would grow into a handsome man. And I was right. You're almost there, aren't you?'

Sometimes the world of adults is so strange. She held out her hand to me. The expression on her face was peculiar, indecipherable, and if I were older I might have understood it and taken flight, but that long-ago afternoon, aged fourteen, I knew no better. Unsure what else to do, unbearably excited, I placed my trembling hand in hers.

She coughed again, cleared her throat with a vile sound. 'Can you hear it, Mike?' Her voice was low and hoarse.

I listened. Nothing, not even the drift of music from the other room. I shook my head. Mrs Miller – Vivian – tugged my hand, drew me down towards her until our faces were almost touching. I smelled her shampoo, her elegant and womanly neck. She had a mole beneath her left ear.

'Please don't tell me you can't hear it,' she whispered.

And I listened again, harder this time. And it came to me, but gradually. There. A droning noise. I didn't move. Mrs Miller coughed, coughed again. She seemed to have something caught in her throat. She hacked wetly a number of times, until she expelled onto her palm a small, damp thing coated in her own saliva.

'Ah,' she said, 'I told you, didn't I?'

And I stared, disbelievingly, at what she had brought up. A bee struggling, with intermittent and querulous fizzing, to free itself from its foamy sac. Tiny cycling legs, sodden fur, wings plastered against its plump body. I tried to pull away, but Mrs Miller squeezed my hand ever tighter. She looked at me with a chilling expression of vindication and despair. And we stared at each other, my hand still clasped in hers, as more and more of the creatures clambered from her nostrils and ears. She opened her mouth and a dozen more made their way across her tongue and teeth. They lolled about in the strands of her hair like drunken mountaineers, picked their way over her cheeks, hundreds of them by now, a miniature army triumphant and overjoyed at the fresh lands they had conquered.

The House of Special Purpose

WARREN WAS UNFAILINGLY polite to his parents-in-law, Marta and Leon, and cared deeply for their only daughter Amelia; still, they despised him, he knew. Amelia denied it, of course, and would become frustrated if he ever expressed his dismay. They were just mistrustful, she said. You would be too if you'd lived in Russia in those days. After all, friends of theirs had vanished in the night, were sent to labour camps, never heard from again. *You'd* be wary. You know, when my mother was pregnant with me, my father was jailed for two months for his religious beliefs. They thought they'd never see each other again. It's a miracle they got out when they did. They don't hate you. It's their way, their manner. They're different. It's, you know, a cultural thing.

This sounded reasonable, certainly, but never seemed explanation enough for the way Marta offered up her powdered cheek for a kiss only to shrink back at the precise moment his lips might have brushed her skin, as if fearful of contamination. His father-in-law was friendlier, but not much. There would be a handshake, an offer of coffee, perhaps even an attempt to engage Warren in a discussion of the cricket (for which he had developed a curious passion) before the inevitable silence while Marta involved Amelia in some feminine business in another part of their gloomy suburban home. Once, not long after he and Amelia had started dating, Warren asked Leon about his time in prison and it was one of the few occasions he became animated. They were sitting side by side on the sofa in the lounge room. Leon leaned in close.

'What would *you* do?' he asked Warren.

It was a good question, perhaps the very best question of all. *What would you do?* Indeed, he had wondered how he might behave if ever caught up in revolution or war: could he maintain his moral compass if faced with arrest? Was he a resistance fighter or a collaborator? Before he could assemble any sort of coherent response, however, Leon raised his index finger with something like triumph and pointed to the ceiling or, rather, to the sky beyond. 'Was simple,' he said. 'I went in there to the prison and I prayed.' He whacked his chest several times with a closed fist. 'It is what my soul needed. It was a . . . test. And eventually God took me away from there.'

At first Warren was frustrated by Amelia's parents' lack of English; he suspected they had incredible stories to tell about life in the USSR before the fall of the Wall. As a teenager he'd been mildly obsessed with the 1915 revolution and had spent hours reading about it and studying the photographs of Tsar Nicholas and his doomed family. Poor Anastasia, Olga, and sickly Alexei in his sailor suit: confined to Ipatiev House, known as the House of Special Purpose, prior to their brutal basement-room execution. Despite anti-royalist convictions, Warren had always felt sorry for the Romanovs, overwhelmed as they were by history's fast-rising tide. Right until the end, they had no idea what was coming. Perhaps it was always that way for those who considered themselves above the law.

Over time, he came to see that their inability to converse was a blessing. Despite Amelia's reassurances, his suspicion that they hated him only hardened. Sometimes, when Amelia was in the bathroom or was otherwise engaged, he was sure Marta and Leon talked disdainfully about him in Russian, and more than once he glanced away from the TV to find Marta studying him intently, her lips moving as if mouthing a curse. There were spiteful glares and conspiratorial chuckles. Warren was certain his avowed lack of religious faith – coupled with leftist sympathies – generated in them a puzzled scorn.

Nonsense, Amelia would say later if he told her about it. Stop being so bloody self-obsessed. As if they would be talking about you.

There were complications with Amelia's pregnancy that were not especially dangerous but would confine her to hospital for the next few weeks until their child (fingers crossed) would be safely born. Then, surely, her parents would warm to him. Their blood would be forever mingled: when they looked adoringly at the features of their first grandson or granddaughter, they would, of course, find themselves gazing into Warren's features and those of all the family members who had preceded him. Blood and water. It was the way it worked. And, indeed, when Leon asked in his rusty English if Warren could help him build a fence around the vegetable patch at their coastal shack, he was overjoyed. Perhaps, at last, a thawing in this Cold War!

The house was in a wild and secluded part of the Victorian coast, not far from Walkerville. He could hear the boom of waves when they pulled up in Leon's ancient Peugeot. The old man had been friendlier than usual on the drive down and, although the language difference was a perennial problem, Warren was encouraged by the odd smile tossed his way. Even Marta, sitting in the back seat, seemed cheerier. She and Leon bantered in Russian, but mostly they travelled in companionable silence, exclaiming occasionally at the sight of a charming old farmhouse or a dead wombat by the road.

As they stepped from the car after the three-hour drive, Marta placed a hand on Warren's forearm. That she should solicit any assistance from him was a rare enough sign of trust, but he sensed this was of a different intent. He felt her strong, Slavic grip and turned to her. Marta was stocky and much shorter than him. She gazed up; in her green eyes lurked an unidentifiable emotion, like the imp in the bottle. As always, a dark scarf was wrapped around her head and knotted beneath her chin.

'Know that you can bear anything with God's help,' she said. Her enunciation was clear and considered, almost accentless. Obviously it was a phrase she had practised (that *bear*) and although her words were vague, the meaning was clear: be stoic, endure, overcome. So Russian! Warren blushed. Clearly he hadn't disguised his anxiety over impending fatherhood as well as he'd thought. Immensely touched by this display of affection, he tried to pat her hand, but she withdrew it quickly, Marta-style, and bustled indoors without another word.

Leon was proud of the place as he showed Warren around. The house was simple and old-fashioned, situated on a small, rather isolated block. The uneven backyard had been levelled off near a clump of ti-trees and this was the site for the vegetable patch. It was a good position, protected from the elements. Leon stamped the ground with his shoes, picking out clumps of grass and flinging them away. He and Marta planned to move here when he retired from the Ford factory in the next few years and it wasn't hard to imagine them growing their own vegetables or gazing from a cliff-top into the winds roaring across Bass Strait.

It was late in the day and an onshore breeze had impregnated the air with salt. Warren wondered about Amelia in hospital, all alone, and was overcome with emotion. Longing, fear, excitement, love. He hadn't wanted to leave her in Melbourne but she had insisted, saying it would be good for him to spend time with her parents. It was only for a day or two. Their baby wasn't actually due for another three weeks and, besides, if anything happened, he would only be a few hours away. Go, she had urged. Don't fret so much about everything. I'll be fine. Just go. And so he had agreed.

Later, he ate dinner with Marta and Leon at the wooden kitchen table. As usual, his hosts said a prayer in Russian prior to eating. As usual, Warren declined to participate, preferring to maintain a tight-lipped silence he intended as generous but was interpreted, perhaps more correctly, as conceited. The meal was beef stew accompanied by peas. Marta was not a good cook. The meal tasted metallic. The relative friendliness of the drive down had been displaced by their customary reserve. There was no TV. He was lonely and felt far away from everything he knew and loved. After eating he phoned Amelia, but the reception was weak and he had to walk around outside with the phone held up over his head to snag a signal. She said she was well and not to worry, but she sounded more distant than ever. The last thing he heard of her before the call dropped out was a television in the background and some laughter, probably from nurses in the hospital corridor.

That night he slept in the spare room, its only decoration a wooden cross nailed to the grey fibro wall. The room smelled of Ratsak and damp. A huntsman lurked in the wardrobe's shadow. Leon and Marta murmured in their bedroom next door. Marta laughed, the sound as strange and unexpected as a gunshot. She and Leon were a mysterious, secretive couple. They had had no children after Amelia. Complications, Marta had said once with a dismissive wave. You know.

One day in the life of Warren Dibkin, he thought grimly, as he tossed about on the flabby single bed and listened to the sea's distant hiss.

The following day he and Leon worked on the vegetable patch. Warren was hardly gifted at this kind of thing but it was pleasing to work with his hands for a change and he thought he'd made a respectable showing. Leon's general contempt for office workers was deep and abiding, but Warren's ability to hammer a nail and operate the drill without mishap earned him, he felt, some grudging admiration. Together they unrolled sheets of chicken wire and fixed them to timber posts already sunk deep into the soil. It was tricky work, but not especially difficult. The site for the vegetable patch adjoined a small but very solid shed packed almost to the ceiling with tinned meats, bottles of water, batteries and other supplies. There was also a low camp bed and a pile of blankets. Probably stockpiling for the nuclear winter. A cultural thing. He smiled. Cute.

Who knew what Marta got up to while the men worked? Occasionally she appeared with lemonade or sandwiches, whereupon they would pause in their labours to eat and rest while she and Leon consulted over the enclosure's design. Marta inspected all the joins, shaking the wire, apparently suggesting improvements here and there. The enclosure seemed extremely secure to Warren, considering the only animals they needed to worry about were rabbits and birds and perhaps the occasional wallaby or fox. He was proud of their work and stood up to shake one of the timber struts. Like all the supports, it was extraordinarily well sunk and didn't budge a centimetre. 'Don't worry, Mrs Lukins. Nothing's going to be able to break through this when we're done.'

To which she actually *smiled*.

After two days the vegetable enclosure was complete and Warren was relieved at the prospect of returning home to Amelia. He had been unable to call her the previous night as his phone was out of power and he had neglected to bring – or had somehow misplaced – his charger.

After a gulag-style breakfast of oats, they prepared to return to Melbourne. Warren cleaned his teeth, washed his face and packed his bag. His upper arms hurt a little from his exertions and his hands were scratched by wire ends, but he felt good. The enclosure was well built, strong, and although he hadn't made as much progress with Leon and Marta as he would have liked, he must have earned some respect.

Marta had been fiddling around at the sides of the enclosure since dawn and now stood expectantly beside it with Warren's puffer coat folded over one arm. When he approached she pressed the coat upon him and directed him towards the shed at the end of the enclosure. Then she handed him a can opener. Obviously, she wanted him to put it with the other supplies. Fair enough. No point having all those tins of food if you couldn't open them.

He was halfway to the shed when he heard the heavy gate slam behind him. By the time he turned around, Marta had

The House of Special Purpose

padlocked it and was waddling back across the yard like an echidna as Leon emerged from the house, his overnight bag in one hand. Warren stood there for a moment. Then he laughed nervously and approached the fence. He called out but Leon merely thumped his chest several times and pointed to the sky. Marta didn't even turn around. Then they stepped inside the house and closed the door. Warren grabbed the wire but was jolted backwards. Fuck! He lost his balance and fell onto his back. The damn fence was electrified. Dimly, as he lay on the hard ground and tried to understand what was happening, he heard the Peugeot rumble to life and drive away.

The Possibility of Water

I DON'T EVEN really know where I first met Eli. She was just one of those people I saw at parties and gigs and bars. I liked her and I didn't care that she was a junkie; most people I knew at that time were junkies or at least partway there, myself included. Besides, I'd always had a soft spot for that kind of woman.

I was living pretty close to the bone that summer, more or less at the start of a losing streak that would go on to last another decade. I lived behind a shop in Brunswick Street and washed dishes in a Greek restaurant. I stayed up late, drank all the time and used dope when I could. At night I crouched in my windy room and carved hieroglyphs into my arms with broken glass, messages to myself, reminders of something or other – my own fucking stupidity, perhaps. It wasn't the worst of times for me; they were yet to come.

It was a searing summer, worse in Fitzroy, where concrete streets exhaled the heat of the day back into the night long after sunset. Couples slept on rugs in Exhibition Gardens and news bulletins warned people to ensure their pets had enough to drink. Old people up and died from the heat. At night I dreamed of luxuriant bodies of water. People talked about the heat all the time, giving it a noise it wouldn't otherwise have. It made neighbours of everyone. On the streets, at bus stops, in taxis. 'How about this heat?' 'Hot enough for you?' Drove me mad.

Eli and I were drinking one night at Punters Club, sort of flirting and carrying on. The music was loud and men were yelling and spilling beer over themselves. The summer excitement was fraying at the edges. The bar was packed with people, with their sweaty faces and their moist, lingering handshakes. But there was Eli, the collar of her man's shirt slightly upturned, like a wink, displaying a shiny ridge of clavicle. Somehow we ended up on the step, trying to catch a breeze. She rolled the most perfect cigarettes I had ever seen, applying herself to the momentary task with girlish concentration. When she complained for the hundredth time about the heat, I took her by the hand and dragged her down the street. It was instinctive, spur of the moment. I didn't even really know her that well, but she laughed and went along with it. 'Crazy fucker.' She tossed her wine glass into the air and watched it smash against the road. 'Where are you taking me, you cad?'

Fitzroy Pool was only a few blocks from the pub but I took her along darkened streets and beneath the graveyard shade of elm trees, just so I could hold her hand.

The Possibility of Water

Rose Street. George Street. Gore Street. Neither of us spoke. It was 2 am, moonlit, an enormous night full of murmur and heat. Cars tooted as they passed. People sat on their porches fanning themselves.

We climbed over the wire fence and plopped down on the scrappy lawns of the pool. We held our breaths. I was aware of Eli beside me, the very heat of her. Nothing happened, no alarms or guards or anything. We looked at each other and shrugged. It seemed too easy, but we were in. 'Wow,' she said against my ear. 'This is *amazing*.'

We waited a minute or two before walking around, but gently, unwilling to touch anything, as if in a church or museum. We didn't speak. Crouched here and there on the lawn and concreted areas were pieces of white plastic outdoor furniture. A pair of goggles was slung over the back of one of the chairs. A towel curled like a fat snake around an umbrella pole. The pool itself was covered by a large plastic tarpaulin suspended above the water and which was retracted by a wheel system at the deep end. This would make it impossible to swim, after all. The tarpaulin shrugged against its tethers in the warm breeze. I hadn't taken this into consideration but it didn't seem to matter; it was enough to be inside the grounds.

Eli wrestled off her shoes and stood silently on the concrete, staring down at her feet. Her hair covered her pale face, a momentary vanishing. I sat smoking on one of the sweaty, plastic chairs. Even through my shoes, I could feel the dull warmth of the concrete, as if the great engine of summer idled below the surface. The entire city had fallen silent, aside from the thick rustle of the tarpaulin and occasional swish of wind through the trees that bordered the grassy area.

Now we were inside, we weren't really sure what to do. I felt even more foolish than usual. Finally Eli padded over to me, cupped my face in her hands and kissed me softly on the mouth with her winey lips. 'You're a genius.' It was easily the nicest anyone had been to me in months. I thought I might cry. She squatted in front of me with her chin on my knees and stared at me for a long time, as if trying to remember who I was, which might well have been the case. Even in the half-light I could see she was stoned. Her skin and hair were silvery. It occurred to me that she had been crying. 'You know . . .?' she began, before looking away over at the shuttered kiosk.

'What?'

She turned back to me, shrugged. 'I was thinking. You remember that smell when you were a kid and you'd been swimming on a really hot day and you lie down on the scorching concrete? That smell of, I don't know, chlorine and . . . *summer?*'

'Yes, and coconut oil.'

She smacked my thigh. 'Yes! And icy poles.' She made pincers of her thumb and forefinger and held them in front of her face. 'Peeling sunburn off your nose.'

'Bombs when the lifeguard wasn't looking.'

'Backflips.'

'You could do backflips? God, I can barely swim.'

'Sure. Brisbane girl, mate. Spent my teenage years at the

beach or in a pool. Under-fifteen freestyle district champ. I'll give you a few lessons, if you like.'

The fact that she had told me this made me bolder than usual. I leaned down, making a face, hoping for another kiss. 'What *kind* of lessons, exactly?'

She fell backwards onto the grass, laughing, and stayed there, staring up at the sky. Someone passing in the street called out and laughed. Then silence again. I tossed my cigarette away and the orange tip shattered against the high brick wall, on which were painted the pool rules: *No running. No bombing.*

'It's a shame it all has to come to an end, isn't it?' she said at last. 'All that . . . you know. All that.'

I didn't know what to say. It was true, I guess, about it all coming to an end and it being a shame. I followed her gaze up to the stars and wondered what sort of sound they made up there, supposing they made any sound at all. Perhaps a low whistle, like a faraway train. 'You know the light from some of those stars has taken millions of years to reach us?' I said. 'Might be light from stars that don't even exist anymore, that have exploded or died or whatever the fuck it is they do.'

She didn't say anything, but moved her foot against my calf in a gesture of reassurance. After a few minutes, she stood up in front of me and ran a hand through her dirty blonde hair. 'Come on, then.'

'What?'

'We going to fucking swim or what?' She pointed with one arm outstretched. 'Retract that tarp, my good man.'

'How?'

'I don't know. Just roll it back or something. Can't be too hard. I *really* need to swim. I feel like shit.' And she wandered away.

I struggled with the retracting mechanism for several minutes, but it seemed to be locked by a metal ratchet. It was difficult to see. I felt mildly ill and there was the tart flavour of bile in my mouth. Perhaps I'd eaten some dodgy takeaway food, but I couldn't remember eating anything at all that day. Maybe some toast for breakfast. Perhaps that was it. I stood and kicked at the wheel thing to try to dislodge the ratchet, but to no avail. I was rapidly sobering up and tried, with rising panic, to remember whether I had any alcohol at home.

I straightened up and lit a cigarette. A breeze ruffled my hair and chilled the sweat on my neck. On it came the smell of diesel fumes from Alexandra Parade. Eli was nowhere to be seen and I doubted I would be able to figure out the stupid tarpaulin mechanism. The whole swimming thing was losing its appeal. 'Eli,' I hissed. '*Eli.*' No answer. Fuck. Where was she? I searched the shapes and shadows of the darkness.

The tarpaulin buckled around the centre of the 50-metre pool. I squatted down and looked across the plastic surface, which shimmered slightly in the moonlight in a parody of water. Another movement. A muffled cry. Her voice. Eli's voice. Shit. She was in the pool. She'd gone swimming under the tarpaulin. There's no way she could find her way out from under there, under-fifteen swimming champion or not. Especially drunk and stoned. Shit. I ran back and forth at the deep end, calling to her, thinking I could at least guide her towards the shallow end. I stepped onto the raised edge, then off. Sweat salted into my eyes. I barked my shin against a banana lounge. Should I go in? Again the lumpy punch from beneath the tarpaulin, this time at least a little closer to the edge. I called out her name, told her to keep going in the same direction. What a disaster. I imagined the police, the headlines, jail, my entire life telescoped into a single idiotic point.

Then there she was, barely a metre away, peering out from beneath a cowl of blue plastic. She was laughing and motioning me to be quiet. 'There's no fucking *water*.' She raised the tarpaulin high over her head to show me. Sure enough, a square cave, its neon-blue floor bruised here and there with middens of leaves.

'Jesus. I thought you'd gone swimming under there,' I said.

'You think I'm an idiot?'

'You scared the crap out of me.'

She scratched her nose and looked behind her. 'You get that tarp thing working?'

'But there's no water.'

Eli stared at me as if measuring me for something. Beads of sweat had formed on her forehead and I could feel her breath on my knee. She held out her hand and I helped her from the shallow end. Together we figured out the tarpaulin mechanism, which wasn't so complicated, and rolled it back, releasing the perfume of warm plastic and old chlorine trapped in there for God knows how long, distilled from a thousand summer days. Neither of us spoke as we bent to the task, which was curiously satisfying, a sort of double-handed rolling. Eli didn't say anything the whole time. She was filled with a weird energy all of a sudden, like she was on a mission.

When we had finished, she strolled the length of the pool, stooping here and there to trail her fingers in the imaginary water, shaking her hand dry each time, and when she got to the shallow end she shrugged off her white shirt, stepped from her jeans and stood there in her underwear. It wasn't fancy underwear like I thought she would wear – swiped, no doubt, from David Jones – but plain blue underwear, practical, like from a Target catalogue. She stood there, skin glowing, rubbing one hand over the opposite arm. After a few minutes she approached the curved metal ladder, turned around and stepped backwards, rung by rung, into the pool.

'You going to join me?' She made a whooshing sound with her mouth as she breast-stroked around the shallow end. 'It's nice when you get used to it.' And laughed with the ridiculousness of it, that thing people say to encourage their friends to join them in water.

Unsure of what exactly I was doing, I wandered down to the shallow end and sat on the lip of the pool. Eli watched me from the corner of her eye as she swam. Finally, I swung around and dangled my feet into the pool.

'Careful,' she said. 'You'll get your shoes wet. Don't want wet shoes, you'll catch your death. You can't swim in your clothes, everyone knows that. You'll drown.'

I hesitated, about to say how unlikely that was, when she came up beside me and rested on the edge, elbows winged on either side of her. 'Come on,' she whispered. 'I'll give you those lessons. But we'd better stay in the shallow end. After all that drinking, and if you're not such a good swimmer and all.'

By the time I'd taken off my jeans and t-shirt and kicked off my shoes, it didn't seem so foolish to be swimming around with Eli in Fitzroy Pool in the middle of the night. She stood beside me with one hand cupped under my chest and observed my freestyle with a professional eye. 'No. Your arm is going way too loose coming out of the water. All over the place. Try and drag your fingertips along the surface of the water – the hand that's coming around – so you get that clean action, like this, see? Be with the water. *That's* it. Yes. Nice and tight. Feel that weightlessness? That's what you want.'

I don't know how long we spent paddling about in that damn pool, grinning like seals, kicking up the swirls of leaves, but it was the most fun I'd had in years – made sweeter, of course, by the fact that I knew it couldn't last. I felt I was somehow unbound from myself. Eventually we scrambled out of the pool and, suddenly shy, stepped into our street clothes, into the other, public versions of ourselves, before climbing back over the fence into the adjacent parkland.

We wandered back to her squat on Queens Parade, which smelled of sour milk. She had the front room. We smoked for a while in the sallow glow from the streetlights outside before falling asleep fully clothed as trucks lumbered past. In the night I felt her childish breath against my neck and finally woke late in the morning to find myself alone. It was already hot and when I staggered into the sunlit kitchen, it reeked of heroin. Eli sat in a wooden chair with one arm folded back hard against her chest. She wore jeans and a white singlet. Her neck was sweaty, her eyes post-coital and her belt was looped on the table; she'd obviously just had a hit.

'Hi there,' she said.

A cat purred and squirmed around my legs. I eyed the spoon on the table. 'Morning.'

'I saved you a taste,' she said in a thick voice and nodded towards the crooked spoon. It wasn't a gift, not exactly, because junkies never give gifts — especially not of drugs — but rather a conclusion of events. 'Thanks for last night,' she said. 'It was fun.'

I was surprised, but knew right then and there that I would remember all this, the night and its subsequent morning, the girl in the kitchen like some creature raked from the sea: that it would be a memory to sing across the years to me among so many unremembered nights and days. And so, I guess, it has been.

I mumbled something and set about having a hit, fiddling with a glass of water and a spoon.

The Very Edge of Things

So I'm lying in the darkness staring into space, listening to the crickets outside and trucks passing on the highway and Julia breathing beside me when it comes to me what I got to do. Fuck this, I think. I'm leaving. She breathes so loudly. I hate her ability to sleep through anything, even what we're going through today. The woman is like a corpse after dark. It isn't only the breathing, of course. It's a bunch of things, wearing me down like water on a rock. But the breathing always gets to me.

It's past 2 am and I feel, believe it or not, even shittier than usual. I'm forty-seven, more than halfway there, probably three-quarters, taking all the variables into account, and we're on our way to visit my brother in Adelaide who's dying from cancer. Barry is four years younger than me and has always been as strong as an ox, but I guess there's not a lot you can do when the Spanish dancer moves in. After all, she got our father as well. The room is stifling, so I slip out of the sagging motel bed and fumble into trousers and a shirt before creeping across the thin carpet.

Friend of mine left his wife a few years ago and said you got to do it before you think too much about it, so maybe I'm taking his advice because it seemed he had a good time after that, aside from those legal difficulties, but that was nothing to do with being a bachelor, that was just bad luck. That, and the thing with the bottle of massage oil and the 'nurse', but that could happen to anyone. Wouldn't happen to me – not that I got anything against that type of behaviour – but, you know, horses for courses. What do you expect, name like Lionel.

Coins and car keys jangle in my trouser pocket.

'Are you coming back?'

It's Julia, of course – poor Julia, my wife of a thousand years. Sometimes she scares the hell out of me with what she knows: things I don't even know myself. Although I can't quite see, I imagine her bleary eyes and long hair like seaweed over the pillow. It's a reasonable question, considering everything that's happening, and I pause for a moment with the frayed edge of the wooden door in my sweaty palm. 'Go to sleep,' I tell her after a while – because what else do you say? – and slip out, easing the door shut behind me.

I wander across the parking lot and stand beside the fence of the crappy swimming pool, which is large enough that the motel owners can advertise a pool but not big enough to actually do anything in, unless you're a child. Beetles are paddling on the blue water, which is lit by underwater lights that throw rippling patterns across the childproof fence. Almost looks beautiful. A gritty wind brings the smell of hot asphalt and the promise of other, better places. It has been a bad day and I'm pretty sure things are only going to get worse over the next week. A bird hoots out in the desert beyond the glow of the pool lights and the motel's neon sign. I look behind, half expecting to see Julia padding across the concrete, but there is nothing, no one. She would be staring at the ceiling of our room, chewing her lip, waiting for me to do whatever the hell it was I was going to do.

I pause beside the car. Where do you go after twenty-three years? The car keys are sweaty in my hand and I am about to get in and drive away from everything when I hear music, and there is something about it, a quality that makes me stop. I follow the music around the back of the Desert View until I find myself standing in the doorway of a room.

Inside are a man and woman maybe in their fifties. Both have seen better days, although they have probably seen worse. They pause in their conversation to consider me, a stranger at their door, a man who has also, frankly, seen better days. A radio murmurs a country and western tune. It seems they were sharing a joke but now, keeping her eyes on me, the woman reaches down and fumbles about on the floor for a shot glass, which she refills from a bottle.

But it's the man who speaks. 'Are we too loud?'

'No,' I say. 'I was just . . . It's too hot to sleep. I was taking a walk.'

The man nods. He has a wolfish look about him, with bristling sideburns and upper teeth that protrude slightly over his bottom lip. With a toss of his head he indicates the darkness behind me. 'Well, you want to take care walking around here in the middle of the night.'

I'm not sure if this is a threat. 'Why is that?'

He throws back his drink and crunches on a piece of ice that sounds like a chicken bone, then points over my shoulder with a knobbly finger. 'Go too far that way and we'll never see you again. This is the desert. The very edge of things. Shitload of nothing out there. Place is littered with old mine shafts, apart from anything else.'

He says all this like a tour guide listing the attractions and I don't care for his manner. Falling into an abandoned shaft almost sounds like an appealing thought, however, and I look behind me. There is very little to be seen, but, after a few seconds, I can make out the dark bulk of an abandoned bus Julia and I noticed when we drove in a few hours earlier. Otherwise, the old guy is right: shitload of nothing.

'Want a drink, then?'

I turn back to them. The woman is younger than him but looks like an air stewardess, you know, the older ones who realise simultaneously the job they chose was not so glamorous and it's too late to do anything better than fly around serving coffee at high altitude getting deep vein whatever-the-hell-it-is? Then I notice the couple are sitting in canvas deck chairs and that the room doesn't appear to be a motel room like the one Julia and I are staying in but more like an abandoned staff quarters. There are a couple of camp beds, an esky and what looks like an old school desk arranged haphazardly in the small space. It's late. I don't really want to have a drink but I'm not in a hurry, so I shrug and step inside the room. 'Sure.'

The burning chill of the whiskey is actually very refreshing and I sit there with two complete strangers as the alcohol squirms into the furthest corners of my body. The room smells like an op shop, although it could be one of the pair; up close, they are more decrepit than I first thought.

'So what brings you out this way?' the man asks.

I take a slug of whiskey, unsure how much I want to let on. It's almost impossible for me to talk about my brother right now so I tell them I'm only passing through.

The woman guffaws into her blouse, then follows it up with a thin smile. She sips from her drink and lights up a cigarette, sucking on it with a kind of venom. She's obviously smoked so many of the damn things in her life that her mouth is pursed as a cat's arse. Already, before she's even said a word, I know I don't like her – although, to be fair, I doubt I would like many people in the mood I'm in.

The man shoots her a look, then turns his peepers onto me. He seems to be pondering something and I don't feel so comfortable sitting there, being inspected by some old guy out here in the back of a motel in the middle of nowhere. One drink, I think, and I'm out of here.

But then, still looking at me like he's never actually seen another white man before, he says: 'Are you okay?'

It's one hell of a question. Does he mean in the head or does he mean am I, you know, above board? 'Am I okay?'

'Yeah.'
'What do you mean?'
'Just a question.'
'Are you serious?'
'Sure.'
'Why do you ask?'
'I want to know.'

I take a squiz at the woman, who is watching all this with interest, sucking every now and then on her fag. She's giving nothing away. The whole scene is like some art film Julia made me watch once. Thing was supposed to be packed full of meaning but made no sense from go to whoa. There's a mechanical cough, and a bar fridge I hadn't noticed before shudders into life.

The old guy picks his teeth with a match. 'What do you call a cowboy with no legs?'

The stewardess *snickers*, but me, I don't say anything. I got no head for jokes at the best of times, let alone right now. But the old guy, his eyes are popping out of his head like he's about to reveal the punchline to the funniest joke in history. Then he says, wheezing all the while, barely able to contain himself, 'A low. Down. Bum!'

The stewardess snorts like a pig. I rustle up a smile and sip my drink, suddenly wishing I was somewhere far away and didn't have to worry about anything.

Nobody says a word for a few minutes until the old guy pipes up and says, to nobody in particular, 'I left *my* wife once,' and I'm about to ask how he knows anything about me leaving Julia and what the hell business is it of his but the woman beats me to it. She chucks down her fag and leaps out of her camp chair and has suddenly gathered all her things together – handbag and coat and smokes – and says, 'Jesus, Frank, not this again. How many times do I have to listen to this story? You left your wife. Get over it.' And so on and so on along these lines for more than a minute, while Frank sits in his low-slung camp chair looking the other way. This is probably some sort of long-practised marriage routine. Believe me, we all have them; it comes with the territory.

I figure I'll take advantage of the commotion to get away from these creeps and their art-movie thing but the woman has blocked the door with her arse so I stay put, meek as a little lamb, trying to figure out where to dump my drink because the whiskey is not agreeing with me, and then suddenly – bam – the woman is gone, leaving me alone with old Frankie, who, I gather, is most certainly *not* her husband. A door slams somewhere and that's it. Now all I can hear is the radio playing 'By the Time I Get to Phoenix' by Glen Campbell and I realise that was probably what triggered old Frank about his wife – *by the time I get to somewhere or other*, whatever the stupid lyrics are. *And she'll cry,* blah blah blah. Enough to make you kill yourself.

And then before I can offer excuses and leave, Frank starts up again, almost as if nothing has happened. 'Actually,' he says in his old man's whine, 'it was a night very similar to this. Summer, you know. And I woke up and couldn't get back to sleep so I went outside. The house was boiling hot, no air. We were living in Sydney then. In Randwick.

And, I don't know why, I got into the car, just a *whim*. And found myself driving away. And it was so nice to be in the car alone, me and the road. There is, I think, a special appeal there – a man alone at night with his means of escape. You know what I'm saying? And I drove until I came to a beach and I walked on the sand for a while, staring out at the dark water and wondering about faraway places and then, I don't know, I got the urge to go swimming. So. I take off my clothes. Hot night. And walk into the water.'

Frank speaks in a manner that doesn't leave much in the way of spaces between the words so it's hard to butt in, but right then I slap my hands down on my knees like we've come to an agreement out here in the bloody back of beyond.

I talk fast. 'Well. Thanks for the drink, but I'd really better be going.'

But Frankie pauses, turns to me and takes another sip. He's got a fleck of white spittle on his lower lip and his scrawny neck shines with sweat and he says, real serious, 'You need to listen to me.'

By now the guy is really giving me the shits. 'What?'

'You heard me.'

He's right, of course, about me hearing him, although I'm pretty sure I don't *need* to listen to anything, especially not this crap. He has a desperate whiff about him. Anyway, he takes my silence as agreement and lets loose again.

'Stone-cold sober, I was. And I walked into the water, past the waves until I . . . lifted off the sand, was lifted off the actual *earth*, can you imagine? It was *wonderful* because I had been so long stuck to the ground and here I was like a balloon being set free. The ground – the shells and sand – who knows how far beneath me. Because that's what happens at the beach. You lift off the actual *earth*. And I floated there in *complete* darkness, at the mercy of the ocean and all the creatures that live in there, the sharks and who knows what. Amazing. And I could hear my breathing, the loudest thing in the ocean. The *loudest thing*. And I floated there, rising and falling, rising and falling. And I thought: "Well, if the ocean wants me, it can take me." And I'm listening to my breathing getting louder and louder and I realise that I've drifted right out past everything. In a rip, you see.'

I'm watching Frank and something happens to him as he tells this story. Right in front of my eyes he seems to age. He sags in his seat. Earlier you could see the guy he might have been twenty years ago, before whatever happened to him happened, but now he resembles an old bunyip with a comb-over. And, get this, I'm actually starting to feel *sorry* for the guy. So I ask him what happened next.

He takes a swig of his drink and gives me a sour, blood-shot look. 'What do *you* fucking reckon?'

I press on. 'What about your wife?'

He looks at me like I'm an idiot, which I probably am, and then indicates the room with his glass. He's drunk and clumsy and his drink slops onto the floor. 'Well,' he says, 'the ocean was larger than I bet on. I never quite made it back, did I?'

By now he's giving off a swampy odour, like leaves in a drain. I actually don't have a clue what he's on about but when he offers me the bottle I pour some into my glass and throw it down the hatch. We talk about this and that until I find myself telling him weird things, incidents that seem so lost to memory that I wonder if they belong to my life at all, even though they must. I can't explain it; it's like confession. I tell him about the time Barry and I stole all the apples from Mr Willow's orchard and chucked them into a neighbour's pool. How we went to the Blue Mountains not long before my sister Mary was born and Dad sat on an ant's nest. The time I dared Barry to jump off the shed roof and he broke his leg in three places. When we went on holiday to Darwin. The time he loaned me ten grand when I lost all my money in that lousy run with the horses. And I weep. By God, I weep.

So me and Frank are drinking all this time, going at it the way that only two middle-aged men at 5 am can, and I lose track of everything until there's a stagger in my step, something hooting in a tree, the taste of stale liquor in my mouth and a roar in my ears. Frank is helping me when I stumble through the muggy, half-lit dawn, and I wake later, hours or days, who knows, still weeping salty tears to find Julia kissing me all over my face and neck. She's sort of laughing and sobbing at the same time and I let her kiss me but it's only after a while that I realise she's saying, over and over and over, 'You taste of the sea. Where have you been, you old fool? You taste of the sea.'

Growing Pain

IT BEGAN TO grow in spring, as I suppose lichen always does. Or does it? Perhaps it's a winter thing, all moist and dark? The only time I'd really seen it before was when I went with my mum and dad to Tasmania last year. We stayed in a lodge and went for walks around the place. There was bright green moss and lichen everywhere, on the trees and rocks and stuff. That was definitely winter.

Whatever. In this case, in *my* case, it started in spring. At first, just a tiny I-don't-know-what, a *nub* I guess you'd call it. Barely noticeable, and in fact it might have been there for a while before I even saw it. A dry lump, becoming more obvious over the next few weeks. I actually felt it before I saw it, a small shape beneath the surface where it was trying to get out. It hurt a little bit, but not too much. I didn't tell anybody, even though I probably should have. It was only lichen, I guess, but it was growing along the underside of my right arm.

I'd been painting my desk green and initially I thought it was a blob of paint, even though the colour was slightly different. I went into the bathroom to wash it off, and under the fluoro light I could see much better. It was the size of a ten-cent piece. I tried to flake it off with a thumb but it clung to my skin like a scab. It was on my triceps and I had to take off my t-shirt, hold up my arm and sort of pull the skin over with my other hand to see it. It was pale green and freckled. I put my nose right up against the lichen. It smelled woody and dark. It frightened me a little but I was also amazed. I had finally discovered a secret about myself.

Then my mum banged on the bathroom door. 'What are you doing in there?'

I quickly turned on the basin tap and yelled that I was washing my hands. I hadn't locked the door and was standing there dressed only in my jeans and a singlet. My mum was always checking on me, ever since my dad died. Always making sure I was okay, coming into my room in the middle of the night to see if I was asleep, stroking my hair. She even picked me up from school some days, even though I'd already been catching the bus home by myself for two years. Completely embarrassing when she appeared in front of the school, waving madly and calling out my name. I knew that she had been reading my diary and that she sometimes went through my drawers. I don't know what she was looking for. She asked me about boys and kept saying we were two girls against the world now so we had to stick together. Anyway. There was no sound for a minute, then she said something and I heard her walk back downstairs. That was close. I knew she wanted to come in and see if everything was all right but I didn't want her to see the lichen. I didn't want her to know.

The lichen grew, but slowly. After two weeks it was around the size of a fifty-cent piece. I checked on it all the time. At school I began going to the bathroom more and more. I would lock myself in a stall, loosen my tunic and touch it with my fingers. I liked the feel of it, this tiny rough island against my smooth skin. The other girls began to laugh at me and held their noses when I walked past. One day Eliza Foster came right up to me in the yard and said, 'Is it true your dad died because of your smell?' and ran off laughing with her ponytails bouncing against her back.

But they were right. It did smell. *I* smelled, but I didn't really care. Why would I want to be like them anyway? I was sort of proud of it, like having a dangerous pet, a python or something. In the dictionary it said lichen was a cryptogamic plant, but that didn't really help me, although I liked the sound of it. I'd always been pretty sure I was adopted by my mum and dad, or they found me on the doorstep one day. That's why I had no brothers or sisters. That's why my dad had said *No more* whenever he talked about me with my mum. Whatever it was, I was special, not of this world. My real family would come to claim me one day soon. I had to be patient.

My lichen seemed to stop growing so fast when the weather got warmer. It made life kind of tricky. I couldn't wear anything short-sleeved so I kept wearing a jumper over my school tunic. Even when it was 30 degrees I kept my jumper on. Not that it mattered that much. Nobody wanted to hang out with me anymore. I sat under a tree with my lunch and watched everyone skipping rope or sitting in groups around the yard gossiping. It was boiling hot but it didn't matter. I had a secret. I suddenly knew what it might feel like to be a superhero.

My mum kept going through my stuff and reading my diary, so I was careful not to write anything in there about my lichen. I only wrote dumb girls' things about boys and my teachers. I pretended to have friends and, after school, told Mum things about girls I didn't even know. She cried a lot at night and always looked like she had just woken up, even in the middle of the day.

One day I found her asleep on the lounge room floor when I came home from school. Her hair was messy and her skirt was pulled up above her knees. She looked afraid when I woke her and she grabbed me by both shoulders. 'What are you doing here? Is everything all right?'

'Yes,' I said. 'Mum, it's four-thirty. I'm always home around this time.'

She straightened her hair and shook her head. 'I meant to come and pick you up but I . . . Goodness, aren't you hot in that jumper?'

'Not really.'

She stared at me. Her face was shiny with sweat, like she'd been exercising instead of sleeping on the floor. My shoulders hurt where she was holding me and I thought there might even be bruises there when I looked later. I wanted to ask her if she was okay, but was sort of afraid of how she might answer.

'Do you miss your father?' she said.

I didn't know what to say. I never knew what to say when she said weird things like this. So I shrugged. I *was* hot. I just wanted to go to my room and change out of my sweaty uniform. And my lichen itched when I got sweaty. I tried to step back, out of her grip, but she held me even tighter.

'Do you remember when we went last year to Tasmania?' she asked in a low voice.

I nodded.

'To that mountain?'

Maybe this was it, I thought. Maybe she was going to tell me something. Maybe she was going to tell me where I really came from and it had something to do with the trip last year with her and my dad. I nodded again. 'Cradle Mountain,' I said.

'Yes,' she said. 'That's the place.'

I didn't think about my dad very much. He died three months ago, of a heart attack after his evening jog. There was a clumping sound from the shower and he yelled out and my mum went in there. I went in after and she was there with the water still running, going, *Simon, Simon,* and I saw my dad all nude and wet, like an animal. His hair was all over the place and his face was grey. He looked disgusting. I stayed sort of behind the door; he never saw me. He was probably already dead anyway. Massive heart attack, they said. Large and heavy, according to the dictionary. Having large volume or magnitude.

But then my mum looked like she was going to cry. Her mouth was wobbling. 'It was fun, wasn't it?' she said at last.

'What?'

'That mountain. It was fun, wasn't it?'

'Yes.'

'That walk around the lake. The snow. Do you remember the cute animals?'

I nodded again.

'Your father loved you, Sophie. You know that, don't you?'

'Yes, Mum.'

I waited for her to speak again but she seemed to be waiting for me to say something. She was scaring me a little. Even so, I waited because I was sure she was going to reveal something about my past, about how I was from somewhere else. But she just nodded and told me I was a good girl and how I should go and get changed out of my school clothes.

My lichen then began to spread more quickly. Another bit appeared under my left arm, the *other* arm and across my belly. The next week there was some on my thighs and behind my knees. Late at night in my room I examined every inch of myself. I ran my hands all over my new body. At this rate it wouldn't be long until I was completely covered. I imagined I would soon be able to disguise myself in any sort of garden or forest. On the weekends and after school I practised climbing trees and being able to crouch absolutely still for long periods, like an insect. How not to blink for minutes at a time. Mum watched me from the kitchen window. She was worried because I suppose she knew it wouldn't be long now before I went back to my people.

She talked on the phone to her friends about me and kept looking through my stuff. She picked me up from school most days now. But I would not be held back, I thought. I would not be held back.

But then, of course, everything went wrong.

Every thirteen-year-old girl knows how to get out of school phys. ed. or swimming classes, especially if it's a guy teacher. Five little words: *But I've got my period.* Always does the trick, always starts them blushing. After all, who's going to argue with that?

But when Mr Davies was away on his honeymoon, the vice-principal, Miss Hamer, took us for sport. Hamer the Hammer. It was hot in the indoor basketball court, as usual, and we were meant to bring our phys. ed. uniform of blue shorts and a yellow t-shirt. I told The Hammer that I had my period and went to sit down on the bleachers with a book. It was where I always sat when Mr Davies took the class.

But The Hammer came over and told me to go and get changed quick smart.

'But I've got my period,' I said.

'So what? You're not sick, are you? Come on, Sophie. Get changed, please. It will do you good to get out of that uniform for an hour.'

'But Miss –'

'Sophie. Right now.'

Some of the other girls were coming out of the change rooms and giggling and pointing at me and Hammer. Eliza Foster was showing off some ballet steps she was learning.

I was starting to get really scared. The Hammer was usually not to be messed with. My lichen was all over my legs and upper arms by now. There was even some poking out around my neck, but it would still be a few weeks before I had fully transformed and I wasn't ready to reveal myself yet.

I thought of something I'd heard some of the other girls talking about. 'But Miss Hamer. I've got *cramps*.' And I leaned over with my arms across my belly and put on a face like I was in real pain. I had no idea what cramps were, and in fact had no idea about periods, other than what my mum had told me last year, but who was to know?

The Hammer was pretty and always smelled a bit like roses. She sighed and looked down at me. I sort of liked her, even though I wasn't supposed to. Some girls said she was a lezzo because she wasn't married, but I'd seen her at the supermarket with a man and she was holding his hand. The man was handsome and dressed like a businessman or a doctor. They were laughing and carrying a loaf of bread and some fancy pasta. I imagined them drinking red wine beside an open fire, with their perfect teeth. They would have lots of children and live to be old.

'Sophie,' she was saying. 'We're aware of what you're going through, but we think it's a good idea for you to start doing some exercise and sort of get back into things. What do you think?'

I didn't say anything. Could they know? The Hammer sat down beside me. 'Your mum is very worried about you, Sophie. You used to be such a good student but your results aren't so good this year. I know about your father and I can't imagine what that must be like for you and your mother, but it might be time to get back on the horse, as they say.'

She went on like this for a bit longer, talking about my dad and everything, how my mum had been in to see her, about how concerned everyone was for me. All the other kids were standing around in groups or fighting over the few basketballs. Occasionally they would look over and whisper among themselves but The Hammer didn't care. She even put her arm around me. I didn't say anything the whole time. I didn't even look at her. The bench we were sitting on was kind of grooved and you could run a thumbnail in the grooves and it fitted perfectly, almost as if that was why they were put there in the first place. I imagined a whole bunch of people in a factory running their thumbs down lines drawn along the wood in pencil.

Somehow Miss Hamer convinced me to go and get changed, even when I told her I hadn't brought my uniform in. I don't know why I didn't hold out a bit better. She sent Emily Croft into the bathroom with me because she had a spare uniform and was about the same size. Emily didn't look very happy about it and some of the other girls laughed at her but I heard Miss Hamer telling them off. In the bathroom she grabbed the shorts and t-shirt from her bag and threw them to me. 'There you go, spaz.'

I don't remember even looking at Emily Croft while I was changing. I decided I didn't really care who knew about my transformation and it would be all over the news soon anyway. She would see. Everyone would see. She sort of stepped away as I took off my jumper and then my shirt and tunic. By the time I had gotten into her gym costume, which was a little big but okay, she had backed out of the bathroom altogether.

I jammed my clothes into a locker and stood by the door, where I could hear what was going on outside without anyone seeing me. Now that the moment had come, I wasn't sure how to make my entrance. Even with all the girls screaming and calling out and the sound of basketballs bouncing off the backboards, I could hear Emily Croft talking loudly to Miss Hamer. I imagined her dragging The Hammer over to the bathroom and the gaggle of girls running along behind, all excited and ready to laugh and scream their heads off.

'Miss Hamer. I think you should see this.'

Petrichor

So many things to recall about the summer I turned sixteen. The drought, an incredible dust storm. There was the relentless heat, cicadas shrilling in the trees like furious little angels, thousands of them, millions maybe, but rarely seen. The way they would unexpectedly fall quiet and how large and spooky was the silence that followed. Most of us, I think, have one such season: days we remember with a disproportionate fondness which allows us to believe that, despite all evidence to the contrary, downturns in fortune are only temporary.

I was alone most of the time in those weeks; school was yet to begin for the year, my brother had left home and my parents were absorbed in their floundering marriage. Some afternoons the sky turned orange with smoke drifting across from bushfires burning along the coast. Occasionally, charred leaves would float into our garden, on which there might have been scrawled messages (of help? of warning?), were I only able to decipher the parchments before they disintegrated on my palm. But the most memorable aspect of that season was when I discovered that by standing on an upturned bucket in our back shed and craning my neck to peer through the grubby louvred windows, I could observe the lovely Claire Dixon as she lounged by her swimming pool. Claire Dixon, almost naked, only three or four metres away. Claire Dixon running a thumb idly beneath her red bikini top, the purplish imprint of elastic on her sun-soaked ribcage. *Claire Dixon*. My God.

My neighbour was no ordinary beauty. She could bowl a mean bouncer in backyard cricket, she understood algebra and, although only eighteen, she used words such as *authoritarian* and *pusillanimous* without any self-consciousness. She was contemptuous of the boys and girls who lusted after her, but she had always been generous to me. A few years ago the neighbourhood brats discovered it was lucky to rub the hump of a hunchback; outside the milk bar they pounced on me, so many of them that I toppled to the footpath like a baited bear. Claire shooed them away and, once I was upright, told me to open my mouth, placing a wad of her part-chewed Juicy Fruit on my tongue as, I suppose, some form of consolation. Between other kids such a gesture might have been one of those acts of sublimated violence for which the young have a gift, but her smile at my craven gratitude confirmed it was one of immense kindness. Sad to say, it remains a highlight of my (admittedly meagre) erotic life. Claire was scornful of most people her own age yet for me she reserved scorn's kinder sibling: pity. And pity, as I sensed even then, is the best a man like me can hope for.

The shed in which I set up headquarters that summer was dim, full of disused gardening tools and household junk. It had been built thirty years earlier by the two Italian families who at that time owned our place and the adjacent Dixon property. The Italians were inveterate gardeners and they shared the shed among their clans. Their children roamed freely between the backyards and, to facilitate this, they had cut into the wall of the shed a low door – at most a metre high – that opened straight into the shady back corner of the Dixon place.

The shed reeked pleasantly of fertiliser and kerosene. It contained a long, scarred workbench, several dilapidated bikes, an old cat bed, a dozen boxes in various stages of collapse, and countless tins of screws and nails. The hateful brace I used to wear hung like a torture device from a hook; the sight of it filled me with panic, like an alarm reverberating in a distant chamber of my heart. I tidied the shed to improve the vantage point from which to admire Claire. With some effort, I arranged a little nest of cushions on the bench. My parents thought I had taken up woodwork and to supplement this misconception I scattered around the place random projects my brother had left unfinished over the years: a billycart, some bookshelves.

'I've started building a billycart,' I told my mother one night, although I had not a clue about constructing such a thing, nor could I see any reason for one.

'That's nice,' she said, staring vaguely through the kitchen window. Then, after a short silence: 'What did you say, dear?'

'A billycart.'

She looked at me. 'Do you think that's wise? With, you know . . .'

My mother usually avoided mentioning my deformity and vacillated between maudlin fretting (coming into my room late at night, weeping drunkenly when she thought I was asleep) and manic optimism ('It doesn't mean you can't do *whatever* you want, you know!').

'I'll be okay, Mum,' I said.

She seemed to think about this for some time. 'Of course you will,' she said at last, although the pilotless yacht of her thoughts had drifted on.

My parents both worked until quite late and, although I was on school holidays, I didn't venture out much on my own; the stares and occasional abuse from passing cars were often barely noticeable but, like pebbles, agglomerated into a substantial burden; one such weight was enough.

Instead, I took the opportunity to prowl through our house, watching the doltish mannequins of daytime TV. Of course I also spied on Claire, who spent most days beside the pool, where she dozed or read *The Shining* as her fingers traced idle patterns in the coconut oil glistening on her belly. Circles, figure eights, tiny squiggles. She played Pink Floyd on her tape deck. Every so often she would slide into the pool and swim a few laps with her sunglasses perched on her nose. Afterwards, she sat on the edge and wrung water from her hair with a look (eyes part-closed, thoughtful smile) of supreme, private pleasure.

Claire's own parents were rarely home during the day, but one afternoon, with a distinct chill, I noticed her father observing her from their kitchen window. Mr Dixon was tall and his face was pinched and gloomy, like that of a fallen priest. He worked in an office in the city. Claire was lying on a lime-green lilo in the water, eyes closed, oblivious to his intense gaze. It was an unsettling scene and I had the disconcerting impression that each of them had unwittingly summoned the other from a nightmare or dream. I don't know how long he had been there when I saw him, but he stood unmoving for at least twenty minutes before his pale face withdrew from sight, as if sinking beneath its own dark waters.

Two or three nights later, my parents were engaged in one of their interminable arguments and, in an effort to remove myself from earshot, I ventured down to the shed. It was after dark, still hot and sticky. As I pushed open the door and switched on the light, Claire slid from the bench where she had obviously been sitting. I gasped, emitting an ugly little grunt of surprise. She looked startled, a marsupial caught in torchlight. Her eyes were red.

'Shit,' she said as she crouched to pick up a half-smoked cigarette from the floor.

I stared at her, she stared back and, in that momentary silence, I heard my mother yelling some obscenity at my father. I shut my eyes in embarrassment and when I opened them again, Claire was standing in front of me.

'Here you go,' she said, holding up the still-burning end of her Winfield Blue. 'This'll make you feel better.'

I took a shallow drag of the cigarette and handed it back to her. She was wearing a thin, Indian-style orange shirt and denim shorts. She was more freckled than I remembered and her eyes were a crystalline blue, as if they had absorbed the tint of the pool water in which she had been spending so much time. Even with a flake of sunburn curling on her nose, she was very beautiful. I tried not to look too closely because, with a face and body such as mine, almost any glance is imbued with defiance or lust.

My parents' voices faded away as they moved to the front of the house. This was how it usually went: my father skulking off as my mother followed him down the hall. Soon, he would drive away, most likely not reappearing until tomorrow, even the day after, with offerings of jewellery or perfume for my mother. So predictable, so tiresome.

Claire finished the cigarette, dropped it to the floor and ground it beneath her sandal. 'My parents fight all the time, too,' she said eventually.

'What about?' I asked.

'Sometimes I'd like to kill him,' she continued, apparently having not heard my question.

'Who?' I asked.

She wound a strand of hair behind her ear, considered me; her expression was very grave and, for a second, she appeared on the verge of revealing something. But instead she nodded towards the shed window. 'I didn't know you could see our pool from here. Why are there cushions on the bench?'

Petrichor

Mortified, I said nothing, merely gazed at the dirt floor. At that moment I heard someone clumping about on the other side of the shed wall, in the corner of the Dixons' yard, by the sound of it, where they piled their garden clippings. Claire's eyes widened.

'Come on, baby,' said a man's slurred voice. 'I won't hurt you, I promise.'

Claire shook her head at me and raised a finger to her lips.

Another stumble and crash, closer this time. The man cursed. His breathing sounded like someone sawing through wood. At last, his muttering fell away. A short silence before I noticed, with a fright, the low hatch opening and Mr Dixon tumbled into our shed. I stepped backwards, almost tripping over the lawnmower.

He squinted up at me and, although he attempted to conceal his instinctive recoil, he was clearly thrown. There was a smear of dirt on his shiny cheek and sweat beaded on his high forehead. 'Oh,' he said with obvious irritation, 'it's you.'

Terrified (of what exactly I didn't know), I nodded. From the tail of my eye, I noticed Claire had slunk deeper into the gloom until hidden behind a stack of sagging boxes full of old books. In an attempt to divert Mr Dixon's gaze from alighting on his daughter, I gestured to the bench, where a wooden fruit box with pram wheels attached was resting. 'I'm making a billycart.'

Still on all fours, Mr Dixon nodded. He looked not at the abandoned billycart, but around the dim shed instead. 'At night?'

'It's cooler.'

'Ah. So it is. You're a bit like the chap from that fairytale, aren't you? Beavering away in the night like Rumpelstiltskin?'

Emboldened, perhaps, by the inverted situation in which we found ourselves (he on all fours, I looming over him), I cleared my throat. 'I'm not sure Rumpelstiltskin made billycarts, did he? I think he wove straw into gold.'

But Mr Dixon appeared not to register my little barb; one evidently needed something blunter to make an impression on a hide so thick and coarse. He sniffed the air, squinted at the cigarette butt on the floor. 'You smoking in here?'

I shrugged, probably looked ashamed; I was, after all, always ashamed.

He considered me and smirked – congratulating himself, no doubt, for not saying *It'll stunt your growth*. Although I was adept at revolving my body to spare people too frank a view of my hump, I sensed him trying to glimpse it, probably in spite of himself.

'Anyway,' he said at last. 'I'm looking for our cat. Damn thing never does what it's told. Needs a . . .' He belched and shook his head.

'Needs a what?'

'A bloody good hiding.'

'Well, I haven't seen him.'

Mr Dixon grunted and peered around again before backing out through the low door. How delightful it was to see someone grub about in the dirt at my feet; at that moment I grasped what it was about me that so appealed (if that was the word) to certain people.

I hoisted myself up and watched through my grimy little window as he staggered past the pool, across the lawn and up the stairs into his kitchen. The slap of the screen door was loud in the night. I felt angry, rattled. Something had happened, but what? I fiddled with some tools on the bench and spun one of the billycart wheels. It needed oil.

After a few seconds, I sensed Claire standing beside me. I didn't say her dad had been searching for their cat – not because she would have heard the conversation anyway, but because I knew Timmy had been run over and killed by a garbage truck a month ago.

'You should come over for a swim one day,' she said after an awkward silence.

'School starts again tomorrow.'

'Oh. Well, maybe come over after school?'

I spun the billycart wheel again.

'The water is really lovely.'

'I'm sure it is.'

'Don't be shy.'

'That's easy for you to say.' This came out sharper than intended; I regretted it immediately.

Claire laid a hand upon my arm. 'I'm sorry, I didn't mean . . .' Her voice faltered, embarrassed, as people often were when they had to refer, however obliquely, to my permanent little companion. Then she rallied. 'Kierkegaard was a hunchback, you know. He was a famous philosopher.'

I recognised the attempt to make me feel better and managed to smile. 'Perhaps there is hope for me yet.'

'Anyway,' she went on gamely, 'if you want to. I'm there almost every day. And I could do with the company.'

It took me two more days (peering from my little hidey-hole after school, trying on and discarding various clothing options like a grotesque little prima donna), but eventually I summoned my courage and squirmed through the hatch into the Dixons' back garden after school one afternoon. Claire seemed pleased to see me – relieved, even – although I must have resembled a monster rising from the undergrowth. She fixed me a glass of ice-cold lemonade, plied me with cigarettes and offered me suntan oil for my pale skin. Miraculously, I managed to feel I belonged by her pool on a searing summer's afternoon.

Of course, I couldn't swim at all (how hellish had childhood swimming lessons been for me: those hours of distilled anguish!) but I was content to sit on the edge of the pool with my feet dangling in the cool water. I wore an extra-large t-shirt to avoid frightening the poor girl to death. We idled away the hours listening to music and chatting. She had finished high school the year before, but was already re-colouring the narrative of her life there with a nostalgic hue. It was the same school I attended, but her experience was so different from mine that she might have been regaling me with tales from the court of Louis XVI; while I was skulking in the library or hiding in empty classrooms, she had been smoking furtive cigarettes behind the bike shed with boys and dancing on the lawn to a cassette player hidden in her schoolbag. I knew there was an entire world taking place somewhere out of view but this was the first time it had orbited so close to my own desolate planet. I was fascinated, appalled, hungry for stories of its exotic inhabitants.

But as glamorous as her high-school years had been, Claire was restless, and longed to escape the city, her family, this country. The suburbs, she said, were only a way station before the future that awaited her in Paris or New York.

'If I had the money,' she told me one afternoon, 'I'd definitely get out of here right now. Definitely. Even go up north and hang out on the coast for a while.'

'That sounds nice.'

Enthused, she sat up on her banana lounge. 'We should *both* get away from this place. My friend Bonnie hitched up to Byron Bay a few weeks ago with her boyfriend. It only takes a couple of days. You'd love it up there.'

Byron Bay. Even in 1983, the beachside town had the aura of Shangri-la: a tropical paradise of topless Swedish backpackers, of mangoes and dolphins.

'I've got fifty dollars my grandmother gave me for Christmas,' I said, 'and I'll probably get more for my birthday.'

'Oh, you're *so sweet.* But we'd need a bit more than that.'

'How much?'

'Dunno. A few hundred bucks, I guess. We could sleep on the beach. Imagine it, swimming all day long, fishing, campfires in the dunes. You can be so free of, I don't know, all this . . .'

Momentarily overcome, I sat there picking at a splintered edge of the pool deck. No one had ever asked me to accompany them anywhere; even my older brother would sneak along the side of the house to avoid taking me to the park, despite my mother telling him to include me in his games.

I heard Claire get up from the plastic banana lounge behind me and walk across the deck. From her vantage point she would have had a clear view of my lopsided back, covered feebly by a sweat-damp t-shirt. I cowered and blushed. She stood next to me (red painted toenails, freckled calf) before launching into the pool and swimming underwater all the way to the far end and back. Her body flickered beneath the surface, a glassy waterfall across her face as she surfaced, the sound of her gasping for air. She shook her head, spattering me with water, with her laughter. I could have stayed by that pool for a thousand years, meek and mild, hoping for a few more such droplets of affection.

Then Claire looked over my shoulder with a strange expression on her face. Their kitchen screen door slapped shut and I swivelled around to see Mr Dixon standing on the back porch with one hand resting on the railing. White shirt, glint of wedding ring. Although his face was shaded, I sensed him staring at us. He didn't move, didn't say anything. I felt Claire's wet hand on my thigh and turned to face her. She stretched up, like a mermaid, to kiss me full on the lips. Her squashy mouth, breasts pressed against my knee, humidity rising from her throat. The shock of it like a delicious, sodden punch in the mouth.

Then she hoisted herself from the pool and wrapped a towel around herself. 'You'd better go.'

I could barely speak. 'What?'

'Time to go. That's all.'

Still stunned, I lumbered to my feet, as elegant as a giraffe, and collected my things. I picked my way down to the hatch in the corner of the Dixons' garden. Glancing back from the shadows, I saw Claire mount the porch steps and go inside without speaking to her father, who stood as if unaware of her, so intent was he on overseeing my departure. Eventually, he followed her inside. I watched the Dixon place through the shed window for several more hours but saw nothing further. My sullen confusion made way for something else. Self-pity, I suppose; grief; the usual.

Night fell. My mother called me in for dinner.

Claire wasn't by the pool the following day when I got home from school, nor the day after. I loitered in the shed listening to the neighbourhood sounds: passing cars, lawnmowers, the corrugated tin roof warping in the heat. Late on the third afternoon I glimpsed her at the Dixons' kitchen window. I held my breath as she stared out, her face like that of a spooky little doll. She waved uncertainly, although it was unlikely she could see me at the shed window from so far away. Then she turned aside, as if responding to a query from an unseen companion, looked out again, vanished. I waited but there was nothing more. The meaning of this strange scene was elusive and in the middle of the night, having pondered it countless times, I wondered if I had seen it at all.

The next day the temperature was forecast to reach forty-three degrees Celsius, one of the hottest days ever recorded in Melbourne. Somehow I managed to convince my parents it was too hot to go to school and, after they had left for work, I scurried down to the shed. There was no sign of Claire, no sign of anyone at the Dixon place. By 10 am the air was limp with heat. Surely on a day such as this she would swim? Something was wrong. I decided to find out what. After much dithering, I crouched to go through the hatch, only to discover it had been nailed shut from the other side. Disbelieving, I tried it several times, but it was stuck fast. How dare he!

I was flooded with inarticulate fury and acted upon a sudden destructive impulse by smashing the stupid billycart to pieces with a hammer. By the time I had finished, sweat poured from my chin and my breath came in ragged clumps. An old mirror hung on the wall of the shed; I normally avoided them as assiduously as I avoided cameras, but on that morning I paused to inspect myself and wallow in the tepid bath of self-loathing. I smoothed my sweaty hair, practised my smile. Mr Dixon was right: I resembled a little goblin. *Like that chap from the fairytale.* I reeled away in disgust, but at that moment a plan formed in my mind.

To get to the Dixon place I had to walk up our street, along Bourke Road, then along the street behind our own. I had never been to the front of the Dixon house but knew which one it was: large, Edwardian, a terracotta gargoyle jutting from one of the eaves. I carried a bag containing clothes, cheese sandwiches and a few books for the journey. Under my arm was a small wooden box of my mother's that contained all we needed to fund our escape. I hid behind an oak tree on the opposite footpath. A boy wearing an Eagles t-shirt purred down the middle of the road on a skateboard. I recognised him as Matthew Barrett, who was a year below me at school. Wagging as well, no doubt. I watched until he hopped off his board at the end of the street and flicked it up into his right hand with his foot. Show-off. I scuttled across the road.

The path along the side of the Dixon house was dark and overhung with branches. The brickwork underfoot was cracked and uneven. I trod as quietly as possible, keeping an ear out for voices from within. By then it was midafternoon, incredibly hot. I was sweating profusely. Strangely, I wasn't afraid; my plan was so perfect in my imagination that it allowed no alternative conclusion to the one I had envisaged. I paused in the shade. An orange butterfly landed on a nearby leaf, where it perched, twitching slightly. A beautiful, fragile thing. I held out a finger, but it took off again, only to fly straight into a large web, whereupon an evil-looking spider darted out from the shadows. I imagined the butterfly's little screams, the *schrick, schrick* of spider fangs being whetted. Seeking to rescue the insect, I reached for it but, to my horror, merely tore off one of its wings.

Which was how Mr Dixon found me: cowering in the shadows with a butterfly wing pinched between thumb and forefinger.

'What are you doing here, young man?'

Idiotically, I held up the wing.

A smile formed on his lips. 'Besides murdering poor insects.'

'It was an accident. I was trying to save it.'

'Ah, a rescue mission?'

I inspected the butterfly wing, which had left a fine dust of scales on my fingertips.

'Can I help you with something?'

I hesitated before speaking. 'Why did you nail the little door in the shed closed?'

Across Mr Dixon's face flitted the same expression I had seen on his daughter's – that of reluctance to reveal something – and I realised how alike they were. He checked over his shoulder. 'Claire begged me not to tell you,' he said at last. 'Do you really want to know?'

I nodded.

'Let me give you some advice.' He lowered his voice. 'Women often mistake desire for kindness, but men: we usually mistake kindness for desire.'

This seemed more like a riddle than any sort of advice, but before I could untangle its meaning, Mr Dixon pressed on.

'Look, Patrick. Claire told me she didn't want you bothering her anymore.'

I reeled. The box I had been cradling under my arm fell to the ground. The world reasserted itself with sudden, bitter clarity: the haze of bushfire smoke, the peeling paint of weatherboards against my shoulder, the tick and whirr of a lawn sprinkler. I heard a querying voice – Claire's – coming along the path and sensed myself gazing about wildly. Perhaps it would be she who rescued me, rather than the other way around? Mr Dixon flicked open the wooden box with the toe of his shoe.

'Dad?' said Claire, coming up behind him. 'Oh, Patrick. Hi. What's going on?'

But her father was gazing at the pile of golden bracelets and necklaces glinting in my mother's jewellery box like a nest of serpents. 'Did you steal this from somewhere?' he asked.

'Of course not,' I said.

'Where did you get them?'

I stood as tall as I could. 'I wove them from straw.'

He looked at me as if I were a fool. There was a gust of cool wind, very sudden, bearing with it the unexpected fragrance of rain on dry concrete and gardens. And then the dust storm struck.

Anyone living in Melbourne that year would recall the storm, which darkened the afternoon as effectively as an eclipse. There are dozens of photos of the massive, three-hundred-metre wall of orange dirt as it rolled over the city and dumped a thousand tonnes of dirt scooped up from the drought-stricken rural regions of the state. Confused by this ersatz dusk, birds twittered in the trees and pets trembled beneath houses or cars. Mr Dixon swore and staggered backwards with his arm over his head. I lost sight of him. The temperature plummeted. There was confusion, exclamations of fear from the surrounding neighbourhood. A woman – Mrs Della Bosca, I think, from several doors down – yelled out. I heard a dog crying nearby, a truly horrible sound, as if the creature were being strangled. Leaves and branches flew about in the wind.

But I sensed other things in the chaos. There was Claire's lovely breath against my ear, her lips soft on my cheek. I felt her caress my hump. 'For luck,' she whispered. I wheeled about, disoriented, but could see almost nothing through the brown, swirling haze. Grit stung my eyes. I covered my face and crouched in the lee of the house.

The worst of the storm was over in ten minutes. Afterwards, there was dirt in our hair and mouths. It coated the grass like a dry, brown frost. Gutters and leaves sagged with it. Mr Dixon loomed up with dust silting from his shoulders. He was repeating something over and over.

'What?' I asked.

'Where's Claire?' he was saying. 'Where's Claire?'

I looked around. The garden was strewn with shredded leaves and plants; the pool resembled a swamp. A sparrow wobbled around drunkenly on the grubby path, its beak opening and closing. But Claire – and my mother's jewellery box – were gone.

Mr Dixon never told anyone about the jewellery box, even when it became common knowledge that our house had been burgled on that strange afternoon. My parents didn't replace it and, perhaps as a consequence of having nowhere to deposit his guilty offerings, my father moved out. My mother died seven years ago after a stroke. Mr and Mrs Dixon moved away. Now only I remain: the keeper of local secrets, teller of stories. Alone, and happily so.

I am still a distinctive figure but, never having had any beauty to lose, I find middle age much more agreeable than childhood or youth. I am treated in the neighbourhood with something resembling affection. People nod to me in the street, offer salutations in the supermarket, assist me discreetly if they perceive a need. I amble to the shops and, while waiting for the traffic lights to change, all sorts of people – kids and adults – touch my back as they pass. It doesn't bother me. We all need some luck, and I am happy to be its wellspring. Besides, we all need that human touch.

And every year or so a postcard arrives – from Los Angeles, from Mexico City, from Jakarta. The postcards are never signed. They bear only a single scrawled quote from Søren Kierkegaard, the same one every time: *Face the fact of being what you are, for that is what changes what you are.*

The Middle of Nowhere

1

Drug addiction is ninety-eight per cent famine, two per cent feast; you get accustomed to bad news. Still, I had no inkling when I picked up the phone on that grim afternoon that what Martine told me would propel us even deeper into the shit. I listened and hung up. The day took on a dreamlike quality, faintly absurd, dark at the edges.

My girlfriend Tess was sitting at the kitchen table when I went back in. She was like one of Schiele's women – all elbows and hair and eyes. 'Who was that?' she asked. 'You look terrible.'

I lit a cigarette. My fingers were like twigs. My inadequacies as a human being were never more evident than when confronted with the prospect of having to console someone. The kettle had recently boiled and steam was bleeding down the window pane. It was winter. It had been winter for years.

'Maggie overdosed,' I said, when at last I could speak.

'Oh no.'

'But she's not dead yet. She's in a coma, on a respirator or whatever.'

Tess stood. 'Oh, fuck. Fuck.'

'In Cabramatta.'

'Sydney? What the fuck was she doing up *there*?'

'Went up last week to get clean. Beach life and all that shit.'

'Is she going to be okay?'

'They might have to turn off the machine tomorrow morning if nothing changes.'

'*Tomorrow*. A machine? Jesus.'

Tess sat down and put her head in her hands. She and Maggie had been friends since high school. I stood at the kitchen door and stared at our crappy garden, which resembled a miniature abandoned city, littered here and there with garden pots and house bricks, the ruins of a wooden chair. It was always like this: when we thought our lives couldn't get any worse, they did.

Things moved quickly. Convinced we might be able to save Maggie somehow, we decided to drive to Sydney. But first we had to score. Phone calls were made, cash counted out on the bed.

2

I sat in Mark and Jill's fetid Yarraville lounge room, waiting for Mark to return with the dope. The place smelled of cat litter. Jill dozed on the couch. Parkinson was on TV, talking to some English dickhead with a private-school haircut. One of Jill's sons came in and pilfered a cigarette from her packet. He was about sixteen, rangy, face set in a permanent scowl. He didn't acknowledge me as he slunk away.

'Fucking kids,' Jill murmured without opening her eyes. 'Suck the marrow from your bones if you give them half a chance.'

A door slammed and Mark appeared and motioned for me to follow him upstairs. By the time I located the bedroom, he had two spoons, a ball of cotton wool and several plastic water ampoules on the carpet in front of him. He gestured to the spare spoon as he drew up his own dope and began to navigate the battered veins on the back of his hand. 'Wanna have a taste here?'

I paused. Junkies almost always came in symbiotic pairs, in which using alone was the worst sort of betrayal. I thought of Tess waiting in the car, but shrugged anyway. 'Sure. Thanks.'

I mixed up, injected myself and sat back to absorb the impact. Those few seconds after a hit offered me a sense of completion otherwise foreign to me. If only it could always be like this. If only the ten seconds after a hit could be expanded to fill every corner of my waking life. Then. Then life would be magical.

I became aware of Mark poking me in the arm. 'Wanna buy a gun?' he was saying.

'What?'

'A gun, mate. Wanna buy a gun?' He held out the item in question, partly wrapped in a tea towel. I had never seen one for real. It was an almost mythical object.

'Piece of cake to use,' Mark was saying. 'See that magazine? With, you know, bullets. Pop it in, snap. Like in the fucking movies.' And then, grinning like a ghoul, he raised the weapon and pointed it at my face. 'I could shoot you right now . . .'

My eyeballs froze.

'. . . not that I would, of course. You're one of me best customers. See that? The safety. Safe as fucking houses, mate. Seven hundred bucks.'

It shocked and pleased me that he thought I was the kind of person who needed a gun. It took a few seconds to locate my voice. 'No. Thanks. I have to go to Sydney tonight.'

Mark stared at me, eyes like holes torn in a sackful of bones. 'What you going *there* for? All that fucking sun. Yuppies. Full of poofters, too. Fucking *full* of poofters.'

'A friend OD'd. We got to see her.'

'Oh.' His eyes drooped and he rubbed his nose. The back of his hand was stained with blood and freckled with track marks.

There came the sound of Jill yelling for him downstairs. I made to leave. It was almost six o'clock. I had been inside nearly an hour already and Tess would be fuming.

'Sure you don't want that gun?' Mark asked again as he rummaged through a pile of laundry. 'It's clean as a fucking whistle, if that's what's worrying you. A bargain, mate.'

Jill called out from the top of the stairs. 'Mark! Get out here, will ya.'

He sagged, momentarily boneless, and the gun, still partly wrapped in its tea towel, dropped into the pile of clothes, soundlessly, as if into water. Then he snapped to and brushed past me. '*Fuck*. What, woman?'

I stared at the butt of the weapon for what seemed a long time. There was a small part of me that had always loved the idea of having a gun. Just for show, that adolescent fantasy of putting it to the head of some drunken thug in a pub, of being the person in the darkened street that others should fear, instead of the other way around, as it usually was.

Outside in the hall, Jill was issuing a lengthy complaint and she and Mark clomped downstairs. Without thinking, I grabbed the gun and jammed it under my leather coat. I went downstairs, where they were still arguing, and hurried to the back door.

'Hey! Wait.'

I glanced behind to see Mark bearing down on me through the stinking kitchen. He was older than me but not someone to be messed with. He was the real deal, a man who had spent lengthy periods of time in Pentridge. Stealing the gun was stupid. Really stupid. Terrified, I fumbled with the doorhandle, but he was upon me.

'Your mate,' he was saying in his tubercular croak, 'the one who OD'd.'

'Woman.'

'*What?*'

'It was a woman who OD'd.'

'You know who he was scoring off?'

I shook my head.

Mark prodded me in the chest. 'Means there's some good dope up there. You find out anything you let me know, okay? Give me a call and we can set something up.'

I nodded and bolted into the freezing night air.

'About fucking time,' Tess said when I got into the car. 'All okay?'

I started the engine. 'Everything's fine. Let's go.'

'You're not fucking stoned, are you? Did you have a taste already?'

'Course not.'

3

Naturally, Goose wasn't ready for us when we swung by to pick him up. Like children, musicians always needed help locating their shoes and socks, their wallets or keys. Tess pushed past him and stomped down the hall. 'Come on, Goose.'

I sighed. 'We're in a hurry, mate.'

'Did you score?'

I searched his stupid features for sarcasm. He had the kind of ravaged, rock-star face adored by women before they knew better. He and Tess had been lovers a few years ago and, although he had dumped her, I knew Goose would take her back in a heartbeat, if only to spite me. 'Yeah,' I said and headed to the kitchen to mix up.

'Bad night for driving,' he said a few minutes later, above the din of rain on the tin roof. 'You sure this is a good idea?'

It was a fair question. I secretly hoped Tess would lose

interest after getting stoned, but she shook her head as she tightened a belt around her upper arm, injected herself, then sloughed off the tourniquet.

Her eyes became sooty. 'No. We got to go.'

Goose hiccuped. 'When are they turning the machine off?'

'Eleven o'clock tomorrow morning.'

'Fuck. What should we take?'

Tess picked a shred of tobacco from her trembling lower lip. 'I'm taking a scarf,' she said at last.

'You think it will be cold up there?' Goose asked.

'No, you idiot, it's . . .'

'What?'

'It's a scarf that Maggie gave me. It used to be hers and she gave it to me because she knew I liked it. It was a present, and I thought maybe it would help her wake up, you know.'

And, as if we doubted her, Tess produced a red, woollen scarf from her bag and waggled it shyly in front of her face.

4

We stopped for a break at a pub in Gundagai and took a corner table after buying beers and a packet of chips. I felt conspicuous among these salt-of-the-earth types, with their dirt-stained fingernails and sun-bleached hats. The beer made me feel sick. I went to the bathroom, where, flushed and faint, I locked the stall and sat on the toilet lid with my face in my hands. This whole expedition was a waste of time and money. The last thing I wanted was to visit the dying – the dead, most likely.

After a while there was a loud bang on the door of the stall. It was Goose. 'Come on,' he was saying. 'Let's get going.'

I unbolted the door to find Goose wild-eyed and gesticulating. As always, he stank of incense and BO. 'There's some guys in the bar reckon they can get us some dope.'

'Is that a good idea? You sure they're not cops?'

'Mate. These guys are *not* coppers.'

'But we don't have much money.'

'Tess and me sorted that.'

When I was ten years old, my father took me to the footy at the MCG. After the game I went to the toilet while my father waited in the crowded concrete walkway. I got confused among the crowds and couldn't locate him in the heaving throng. As instructed a thousand times by schoolteachers and parents, I waited patiently by a wall for the crowd to clear and for my father to find me. I was afraid, nearly crying. The hot-dog stand was closing, drunken groups of men staggered past, armpit to shoulder, like unseaworthy vessels. A small man appeared and asked me gently whether I was lost and needed help and would I like to go with him? The man had eager, beery breath and a shaving cut on his right cheek. I was unsure how long he had been there with one hand outstretched, as if offering me an invisible gift or, perhaps, waiting to take something from me, and, as I stood in a cold bathroom at the back of the Gundagai pub inhaling the scent of urinal cakes and chip fat, I was reminded of that long ago day.

I nodded and followed Goose into the bar.

5

We trailed the bobbing tail-lights of the ute along the highway, then onto a dirt road. The Corolla was my car, but Goose was driving, hunched grimly over the wheel. Dust billowed up around us.

I leaned forward. 'How far is this place?'

'Couple of kays, they reckon.'

'Do we know the way back to the highway?'

Tess turned in her seat. 'Jesus. Relax, will you.'

The car swerved. There was a soft thump against the undercarriage.

She squealed. 'A fox. Was that a fox?'

Goose nodded. They dissolved into giggles.

I looked behind us but there was only the pale ribbon of road vanishing into darkness. After fifteen minutes we pulled up at a two-storey weatherboard house with a sagging porch. Wrecked cars huddled on the lawn. Two guys stepped out of the ute, waved for us to follow, then entered the house. Goose cut the engine. A frog gulped somewhere nearby. We tumbled from the car, Goose and Tess now in charge, me scurrying along behind like their little brother.

One of the guys from the ute appeared in the dim hallway and led us through to a kitchen out the back. He was young, rat-faced, with a lick of black hair across his eyes. His gaze lingered on Tess's tits. 'Wanna beer or something? A cone? Jimmy'll be down in a sec.'

But Goose was all business. 'Jimmy our man, is he?'

Ratface nodded. Another man appeared in the kitchen but I couldn't tell if he was one of the two from the ute or another guy altogether. He was a big meathead, with hairy forearms. Meathead pulled a beer from the fridge, cracked it, downed several loud mouthfuls and let out an almighty burp. 'Ah. Good fucking stuff. You want one?'

Tess sighed. 'Actually, mate, we're in a hurry. A friend of ours is in hospital and we need to get to her, so –'

'She your girlfriend?' Meathead asked Goose.

'No. She's with him.'

Meathead looked at me as if he could scarcely believe it, before swivelling his gaze back to Goose. 'What's that tatt there, under your sleeve?'

Goose rolled up his shirt to display his forearm, and a mini-skirted nurse brandishing a squirting syringe. Meathead grunted appreciatively and swigged again from his can. He winked at Tess. 'Got a few of me own, you know. Hidden away. I'll show you 'em later. *Mate.*'

Goose checked his watch. 'Look. Sorry, but we are in kind of a hurry, as we said . . .'

Meathead picked something from his teeth. 'Okay. What do youse want again?'

'Just what we talked about at the pub. Is it Jimmy we need to see?'

Meathead stuck out a paw. 'Nah. Jimmy's not here. Give me the cash and I'll run it over to him and pop back with what you need.'

Ratface sucked on his bong with a throaty gurgle.

Goose smiled nervously. 'Um. Not sure how you do

things here, but if I'm gonna hand over eight hundred bucks, I need to see the gear first.'

Meathead drained his beer, crushed the can and dropped it to the floor. 'Come on, mate. Hand it over.'

My knees began to wobble. We were a long way from anywhere. Nobody even knew we had left Melbourne. And there was no fucking dope.

Ratface put his bong on the table. Goose stood. 'No, it's okay. There's obviously been a misunderstanding or something . . .'

The next bit was a blur. Ratface was on his feet. Meathead shoved Goose back into his chair. Tess protested. Another chair was clattering to the floor and then I was standing, saying something like *Watch it* or *What's happening?* I remember noticing the cold floor through the soles of my shoes and thinking I really needed a new pair. Meathead was poking Goose in the chest and Tess was gesticulating, and it was then I saw someone outside looking in, before realising it was, in fact, my own reflection in the window, hovering like a small, sallow moon in the darkness.

Then Ratface's little mouth opening and closing, opening and closing. 'Holy shit. He's got a gun. Phil, he's got a fucking *gun*!'

And he was right; I had the gun in my hand. Everyone stopped. Meathead stepped backwards. 'Whoa there,' he said to me. 'We're only kidding ya.' There was a curious pause. 'Bet you don't even know how to fire it, do you, mate?'

This was true. I wondered about the safety catch. My teeth ground against each other. There was a flat crack and my hand – the one holding the pistol – jerked and I thought that someone had knocked it, even as Meathead staggered backwards saying, 'Ah, fuck, you *shot* me, ya cunt.'

And then Meathead was sprawling against a cupboard with blood oozing between his fat fingers. I don't quite know where my new-found authority came from but I heard myself tell Goose and Tess to get outside and start the car.

By the time I dived into the passenger seat, Tess was weeping in the back seat. Goose wrestled with the steering wheel. The car skidded and bucked. Someone, perhaps even me, swore. The car stalled. Ratface and Meathead appeared on the porch, waving their arms about and shouting. Goose fiddled with the ignition. A crack. Tess yelped. 'They're shooting at us! Fuck. Go.' Then the car was careening out of the driveway. Another shot. 'They're coming after us,' she said. 'We're dead.'

Trees blurred past. Objects reared from the darkness, illuminated momentarily by the approaching headlights before vanishing. A road sign, a wire fence, the bobbing light from a distant farmhouse. Tess was still yelling and I think Goose was as well but the only thing I recall with any clarity was the sense of having been let in on a great and terrible secret. *My God*, I thought, *so that's what it's like to shoot someone.* And there, in the passenger seat, as we barrelled through the night, I almost laughed.

We sped along dirt roads for what seemed like hours, Goose crunching through the Corolla's gears and sliding through corners until, miraculously, the lights of the tailing ute vanished. We pressed on – passing no cars, seeing only the glimmering eyes of animals in the night – before coming to rest beside a paddock. Goose cut the engine and we sat there in silence, smoking and chewing our nails.

6

When I woke, my shoulders were crunchy from sleeping against the car door. It was cold. My breath fogged in the weak light. I heard the call of a crow, like the brief cry of a falling infant. Then something more sinister, a clumping about right outside the car. Huge and heavy breathing. Images from the previous night flickered in my mind's eye and I wondered if I had the heart – or whatever part of me I had used – to shoot someone again.

Tess moved in the back seat. 'What the fuck is that?' she hissed.

I reached for the gun and peered cautiously through the fogged glass. Impressionistic splodges of colour, then something much closer, a lumbering darkness, a giant head. Eyes.

Tess laughed. 'A cow. It's just a fucking cow.'

I wiped the glass clear with my sleeve. Sure enough, right in front of me – so close that were the window open I would be able to pat the damn thing – was the massive head of a cow, looming with mouthfuls of grass torn from the ground. I laughed with relief.

Tess and I stepped from the car and the cow backed off with a snort. We lit cigarettes and looked around. We had come to rest in a grassy clearing beside a rutted dirt road. There was a farmhouse in the distance and a pretty weatherboard church a few hundred metres away through the trees.

Tess drew hard on her cigarette. 'What time is it?'

I checked my watch. 'Nine-thirty.'

I rubbed my freezing hands together. We were stranded God knows where with a gun that, for all I knew, had killed someone. No one becomes a junkie by accident; it takes a certain amount of determination. Sadly, that determination was never quite enough to stop being a junkie, and for years I had been in way over my head. The whole thing was depressing. I blew a smoke ring and watched it unravel as it glided away on the cold morning air.

Tess pointed at something. 'Look.'

Beside the church, almost indiscernible among the grey trees, was a crowd of about fifteen people standing in a loose circle. We watched them for a few minutes and then, as if drawn on a current, picked our way across to them through the broken headstones. The cemetery smelled of damp grass. A few of the mourners glanced up at our approach before turning back stoically to the casket in the open grave. The service was coming to an end. The priest was reading something from a Bible. We stopped at the edge of the gathering as it broke apart. Someone was weeping loudly, inconsolably, a terrible sound. Mourners tossed handfuls of dirt and small items into the grave and left in groups of two or three, nodding vaguely to us as they passed.

An elderly woman was the last to leave. She approached us and placed her hands on Tess's shoulders. The woman was short, powdery. 'It's all right, love,' she was saying. 'She was ready to go. She was in so much pain. It's better that way. I know it's hard, but do you know what?'

It was only then I realised that it was Tess who was weeping so loudly. Her shoulders were convulsing and her face was furrowed and wet. She was nodding and trying to say something but the only sounds she made were inarticulate sobs of grief.

'You were her favourite,' the old woman went on. 'Her absolute favourite. She talked about you all the time. Goodbye, dear.'

Before leaving, the woman looked at me with a gaze that was like a spotlight across my frozen cheeks. She gave my upper arm a quick squeeze. Then we were alone, except for the sexton waiting a respectful distance away.

Tess continued to weep for several more minutes before she composed herself and kneeled at the edge of the grave. Cold in my denim jacket, I waited, wiggling my toes for warmth. The polished coffin lid was spattered with clods of earth and photographs, a book of poetry and an old hat. Weird to think that someone was inside that box. A dead person. A sob caught in my throat. My face tightened.

After a while, I kneeled beside Tess on the muddy ground. Uncertainly I put my arm around her shoulders and pulled her closer to me. She didn't resist. 'I'm really sorry about Maggie.'

She unwound the scarf – the one Maggie had given her – from her neck and considered it for a few seconds before tossing it into the grave. I checked the gravedigger wasn't looking, took the gun from my jacket pocket, wiped it on my jeans and allowed it to fall into the hole.

Tess sniffed. 'What the hell were you thinking? Where did you even get that fucking thing? Do you think that guy died?'

I shook my head. I didn't want to talk about it. I didn't want to talk about anything. We kneeled in silence for several more minutes before standing and walking back to the car. Goose was still asleep inside.

'Where the hell are we?' Tess asked.

'God knows.'

She sniffled and looked at me with red eyes. 'We'll never make it now, will we?'

'No.'

'We really fucked up, didn't we?'

'Yep.'

'Got a smoke?'

I shook one loose from the packet and lit it for her.

'Any idea how to get back?' she asked.

'None at all.'

And we stood there for some time, it might have been years, trying to decide what to do as the sun rose behind the trees.

The Other Side of Silence

I'll admit that I wanted him dead and would gladly have done it myself, given the opportunity. Sometimes I wonder about the days before fingerprinting, before CCTV, forensic analysis and Google Earth; how easy it would have been to do away with someone.

In the modern, *friendly* courtroom, where the sentence was handed down (a mere two years! On a prison *farm*!) it felt as if the entire world were a poorly constructed jalopy that had lost a wheel, only to continue careering down the asphalt, chunking up sparks as it went. After sentencing, the judge, a chap called Roger Hilliard, a fellow I actually knew of through friends of friends, plumped his papers and swept from the courtroom, steadfastly refusing to meet my eye. Well might he have been ashamed at his part in a system that had so obviously failed to punish adequately the man who killed my daughter.

Meanwhile, the dolt in question exhaled noisily like the

pig he was, turned to his dumpy wife and smiled a tight smile of *Oh well, honey, it could have been worse*, while she dabbed at her mascara. They referred to the crime as an accident, which was true *technically*, but, let's face it, nobody forced the man to drink twenty glasses of beer, jump in his ute and speed through the first red light he encountered. Nobody had a gun to his head.

Marie and I had struggled to have a child at all and, as a result, Carol had been much hoped for, much loved and occasionally much spoilt. It is true that parenthood erases utterly the life you lived before, but even after the child has departed, it is impossible to return to the things that might otherwise have occupied your time. The massive space that develops in one's heart to accommodate a child does not, womblike, shrink, after the child is gone. For a long time, both Marie and I woke early in the morning and wondered what to do with ourselves. What we did before Carol came along had, in the early days of parenthood, been the question we asked ourselves. Now the question was: what could we do now she had gone?

I felt Carol's loss deeply but it was Marie who mourned for her most elaborately. She visited her grave regularly, often alone, and hoarded her personal items for longer than was necessary. They had been the closest mother and daughter I had ever had the pleasure of knowing, distinguishable from a distance by their manner of walking arm in arm in a clumsy but touching pas de deux. Marie moved a framed photo, in which Carol was at her most beautiful and most assured, to different locations throughout the apartment – now on the bedside table, now the bookcase, now the kitchen bench – as if she might give our beloved daughter animation. More than once she dialled Carol's number for a chat, only to realise, with a horror that never really dims over time, that she was calling a number now registered to a complete stranger. I'd have done anything to ease her pain and it is no exaggeration to say that I gladly would have swapped places with Carol – stepped off that kerb into the path of the speeding truck – if it meant that she could have lived her life through to its natural conclusion. Grief is not one of life's human *journeys*, as those saccharine New Age mystics might tell you, nor is it a destination; rather, grief is an entire continent, apparently endless, with its very own topography and foreign tongue, a nation in which one loses one's passport and papers and must spend the foreseeable future.

After the hullabaloo diminished, Marie and I resolved to take a few weeks away from our interfering families and the inevitable follow-ups from the press. On a whim we decided to revisit the coastal town of Mallacoota, where we had spent two weeks thirty years earlier, before Carol was born. It was a place we remembered with great affection, a place where our sorrows might even be unknown to the general public and thus more easily forgotten. It was a simple and isolated place. There was a time when, having been elevated to such lofty heights in our personal history, Mallacoota was used as a sort of touchstone when we assessed the worth of other destinations. We would shake our heads and say – laughingly, but also with complete sincerity – things like: 'The Dalmatian Coast was nice, but it was no Mallacoota.'

In this way, the humble Victorian seaside town assumed an iconic status and I suppose that was part of the appeal of revisiting: the hope that, after all the tragedy of the past few months, the solitude and peace might offer us solace, rejuvenation, a chance to set the world to rights. And so it did, but in the most peculiar of ways. Revenge, I discovered, is merely the wish that a particular person not experience the life denied someone you have lost.

We arrived at night, as we had thirty years ago, located the house we had reserved several days before and received our instructions from our landlady, a gnome of a woman with energetic eyebrows that tumbled across her forehead like a pair of gymnasts. She activated the utilities, explained the neighbourhood and showed us how to work the automatic garage door. Before she departed, she left a photocopied sheet with a map and a list of names and phone numbers for various services we might require in the township: boat hire; takeaway food; massage and so forth. She assured us we would be undisturbed and urged us to call her should we require anything at all.

The house itself was large and comfortable, almost as tastefully appointed as our own apartment. We unpacked our supplies, and it wasn't long before we were nestled on the couch with a fire blazing in the hearth and glasses of red wine cradled in our hands. The silence was deep and tranquil, interrupted only by the occasional crackle and pop from a burning log or the call of a bird in the night.

That night we lay in the unfamiliar bed under heavy blankets and stared into the darkness, into the past and into the future, such as it was. I wondered what the man who killed our daughter was doing and hoped that, at that precise moment, 3.15 am, he was being abused in some dreadful fashion by a prison lunatic.

Over the week we began to recover a little of our former selves. We both knew it would be a long haul, but at least there were the beginnings of adjustment. We would rise early to eat toast spread with local marmalade on the sunny lawn, overlooking one of the series of lakes fed by the nearby ocean. Contemplatively, we watched boats tacking back and forth in the late afternoon breeze. Arm in arm we walked the pier to inspect the catch of the men and boys fishing there. Marie, with her binoculars always to hand, sought out birds, checking them against a book bought especially for the purpose of identification. At night we watched DVDs or read quietly, rising now and then to prod the fire or refill our wine glasses. The view of the horizon and the nippy sea air, carrying on it the scent of distant places, combined to make us feel more positive, more hopeful. Even Marie seemed to display flashes of her former self.

There was, it was true, an occasional melancholy that settled upon us when we were reminded of Carol's absence – often by the most obscure object, a TV show, say, that we knew she would have enjoyed, or a jumper in a local shop she might have liked — but these episodes became more manageable, almost *companionable*, like adjusting warily to the presence of a stranger.

The peace and quiet came to a halt, however, when a group of about fifty hooligans descended on a neighbouring house one night and proceeded to have the loudest party I had ever heard. I had observed them with some foreboding as they arrived by the carload throughout the afternoon. Marie chastised me for being a fuddy-duddy when I expressed the fear they would disturb our solitude, but my fears were well founded. From 8 pm, the night overflowed with a brew of the most appalling thudding music, the screech of drunken women and the hoarse arguments of young men.

At first we tried to ignore it and passed the evening as we had passed the previous seven. I told myself that it was all fair enough, that I myself had most likely kept a few people awake during my more reckless years, but as the hours wore on, I became increasingly agitated. As a man, one feels the burden of having to 'do something' on such occasions, so when 2 am rolled around and the noise gave no indication of abating, I got out of bed and dressed.

'But what will you do?' Marie asked.

I shrugged in the darkness. 'Ask them to stop. Have some consideration for us.' It sounded pathetic and I knew it.

Marie sat up. 'Well. Be careful. Don't say anything foolish, Clive. Please.'

I pulled on my sandals and reassured her but she insisted on getting out of bed and observing through her binoculars. I knew the set of her voice and declined to talk her out of it, even as I thought it pointless.

The two properties were separated by nothing more than a large stand of pine trees and as I padded beneath them and out into the party's penumbra of light and noise I felt as if I were entering an obscure circle of hell: people thronged about in various states of undress and evident intoxication; girls huddled here and there on the lawn. The music was obviously, unbelievably, even *louder*. I was aware of partygoers observing my progress with slightly bemused contempt, as they might a dog walking on its hind legs. And yet I pressed on.

The house was larger than the one where we were staying and was lit up like a film set. People danced. A tide of youths ran past me, yelling and calling to each other. They all shone from a day in the sun and were smartly dressed, obviously enjoying the hospitality at the beach house of one of their parents. I crossed the lawn, ducked beneath a tangle of coloured lights strung across the terrace and stood on the threshold to a living room.

In the short walk across the lawn I had run through a variety of scenarios, all of which involved me emerging victorious from whatever altercation I was about to engage in, but now I was here, in the thick of it, my resolve ran from me like water. I gazed around at them, at the way they sprawled on couches and bounded up the stairs. It was horrifying in a way that only came to me slowly as I stood there being jostled by passers-by; what galled me most, I realised, was that they all had life, were fairly bursting with it, while my daughter, dear Carol, lay crumbling in a box in the earth, cold and alone, miles from us. A couple smiled at me as they squeezed past. I wondered if Marie was observing me through her binoculars and could feel my masculine pride under scrutiny; I retreated nonetheless, back to our temporary home, back to bed.

'What happened?' she asked when I was under the covers ten minutes later.

'Nothing, really.'

'You didn't talk to anyone?'

'No.'

'How old were they?'

'Were you not watching?'

'Yes,' she admitted.

'Well. They were in their mid-twenties, I suppose.'

Marie drew a breath. 'Carol's age.'

'Yes. More or less.'

With seemingly endless goodbyes and slamming of car doors, the party finally dissolved shortly before dawn. Still, Marie and I got up early and set out for a walk not long after sunrise. The day was misty but, if the past week were any guide, would clear up by midmorning. We didn't mention the party in detail, only to say how tired we were. I myself felt positively ancient, beyond living. We walked along the road for a short distance before cutting down a sandy track to a headland that looked over the curving beach. We stood and the wind whipped about our legs and shrilled through the stubby banksia. Marie peered through her binoculars out to sea in an effort to spot some bird or other she hadn't yet ticked off her list. I huddled in my woollen coat and watched the progress of a person surfing far below. A man, I eventually discerned, who determinedly paddled out on his board through the roiling surf and waited for the right wave to ride back in to shore. He didn't seem particularly good at it and was dumped repeatedly, often before he even had a chance to ride his board for more than a few seconds.

I found myself willing the surfer on, urging him to stay upright longer, and felt unaccountable disappointment at his failures. After fifteen minutes of this, he appeared to get into difficulty. The board that had been lashed to his ankle came free in a smashing wave and he found himself past the breaking waves in deep water, flailing somewhat, his black, wet-suited arms waving about in the foam like a beetle drowning in milk. A quick scan revealed there to be no one else on the beach, indeed no sign of humans at all as far as I could make out, even though I knew the township was not far beyond the scrubby dunes. I tapped Marie and pointed to the surfer.

She swung her binoculared gaze to where I had indicated. 'Clive. Have you got your mobile phone?'

I fumbled through my pockets and located the damn thing, as small as a matchbox.

'Call someone. Call triple-0. Quickly. They can probably get the rescue people out there. A boat. Save him.'

I was wrestling with my phone, struggling with the tiny keypad, when Marie, still with her eyes glued to the binoculars, placed a hand firmly on my forearm.

'Wait,' she said. A pair of gulls wheeled down out of the sky, landed on the grass nearby and shrugged their wings. 'It's one of them.'

I managed to unlock the phone and was dialling. 'What? Who?'

Her voice was astringent. 'One of those . . . *arseholes* from last night.'

It was extremely rare for Marie to swear. Even throughout the trial, she had managed to withhold her anger, though I could detect its presence by the set of her mouth. I waited with phone in hand. The wind buffeted us where we stood, out there on the headland, exposed to the elements. We didn't speak a word. I was aware of Marie, my beloved wife, steadying herself against the gusting wind. I was aware of her short, brown hair flicking this way and that, of her unzipped jacket flapping about, as if the fingers of the wind were searching for something hidden about her person – some grief, most likely – that might be taken away and discarded. Marie kept her hand on my arm. Her grip tightened slightly, almost imperceptibly. I understood at once what she was communicating.

It was then I saw us from a distance – as one of the wheeling seagulls might have – two old things in their all-weather jackets on a windswept bluff, diminished by nature. I dropped the phone back into a pocket and we watched, Marie and I, somewhat *greedily*, I am ashamed to say, as the surfer struggled against the tide, his head disappearing and reappearing within the creaming waves, his dark mouth, visible even at this distance as it opened hungrily for air, until he reappeared no more.

By the time we made our way down to the sand half an hour later, a small crowd was hovering around the fellow's body like birds. As if she had read my mind, Marie coughed into her fist and began to speak above the sound of the wind. 'Do you know,' she said with some satisfaction, 'that the collective noun for herons is a siege? A siege of herons.'

Our progress was unwieldy; the sand was heavy and thick, our old bodies tired. We huddled and bent into the whippering wind until we approached the group, who were by now standing around with their arms across their chests, obviously waiting for the ambulance or police. We did not stop. One or two of their number looked up but if they recognised me from the party the night before they showed no sign of it, and we offered no greeting of our own. We kept on and by the time we left the beach, stamped our shoes free of sand and went into the house – now quiet, now peaceful – I expect the ambulance would have arrived.

The Mare's Nest

'Don't tell anyone what happened here,' were my father's last words to me – to any other human being, as far as I know. 'Do you promise?'

'Yes.'

'They won't believe you and then they'll lock you up. Never tell a soul.'

And then he let go of my hand.

One long-ago dusk my father and I sat on a low hill overlooking a sports field. The air was raw and cold. I became aware, all of a sudden, that he would die one day, that it would be before I ever really got to know him, and that his death would be like something unravelling after being held together with sticky tape and paper clips. I felt an immense sadness, as if my twelve-year-old self were already casting ahead to the moment when I would recall this evening with fondness, with amazement and with regret.

The soccer nets sagged and the white lines marked on the grass were faded to near invisibility. As it darkened, the grass would come to resemble a square lake, an impression intensified by the muddy smell blown up in the wind, and the susurrations of the trees, which were easily mistaken for the lapping of water. My father brought me here often, because it was from hereabouts that his own father was taken fifteen years ago.

Although the police never solved the mystery of what happened to my grandfather, this was the word my father always employed so it became the one we used in the family. *Taken*. The word was now an heirloom, much handled, although its value and use were uncertain.

On that night my father was talking in his quiet voice about a workshop near our house that cast medals and statues, the kind of awards given out at local tennis carnivals and flower shows and the like. This was an old theme of his; he believed the failure of so many marriages in the suburb – not to mention the suicide of old Mr Granger and the alcoholic tendencies of Megan Talbot at Number 16 – could be attributed to the workshop.

'I know people think I am foolish,' he said, brushing dried mud from his trousers, 'but I have been there at night. I have wandered down and there is often a strange smell. Toxic. Toxic smoke comes out of that chimney at night and I believe there is something evil in it, some sort of – you know, some sort of poison. We should get it investigated. Get the authorities onto it.'

The authorities. This was another theme of his. He talked

often of alerting the authorities to some indiscretion or other but, as far as we knew, he never actually approached anyone. His complaints were regular but deeply regretful, as if in the very process of making them, he was already aware of everyone's unwillingness to take them seriously, a misjudgement for which we all would dearly pay.

'There are things, you know, that... defy description,' he continued as he plucked blades of grass and rolled them between his fingers. 'The afternoon that my father was taken was much like this, actually. The trees, the sky. Before it happened I had an odd feeling that only later I realised was a... *premonition*, I guess you'd call it. I thought at first they would bring him home again. I was certain. And I thought they would come back for me. But it's been so long now. He held out for a long time.'

For many years afterwards, when I was playing with my sister Peggy in the garden, I would glance up and see my mother observing us from the kitchen window, watching us for nascent signs of our father's madness, as if it were a weed she might pluck before it spread. She would come into my room late at night and stroke my hair, for what sometimes seemed like hours. She made sure the bedroom windows were always locked. On these occasions I pretended to be asleep, but I could sense her tears. Checking I had not yet followed my father, wherever it was he had gone.

He was convinced there were scraps of meaning to be found between the cracks of consciousness, the way one might find tiny pieces of paper – on which would be scrawled secret messages, codes, formulae – rolled into balls and stuffed into the fissures of a brick wall. He listened out for distant voices and would spend interminable hours slowly rotating the radio dial in the hope of finding transmissions intended for him alone.

After he had gone, my mother and I found dozens of small notebooks in which he had written the meanings of obscure words that interested him, along with recondite facts he gleaned from God knows where. None of us had ever seen these books before or indeed seen him writing in them. We could only guess that he did it late at night when the rest of the household was asleep. I imagined him slouched over our kitchen table, eyeglasses perched in an approximation of a professorial bearing, laboriously writing out words he had looked up in the dictionary or asked someone the meaning of. It was an image that made me weak with sorrow.

Occluded – closed off. Beans can be used as a homeopathic charm against witches and spectres. The word 'panic' comes from the god Pan. A mare's nest is an extraordinary discovery. Obligato – a persistent but subordinate motif.

My father was an ordinary man but aspired to be something more. Each time I visited him in hospital he regaled me with a new fantasy. He claimed to have invented clothes pegs, to have somehow caused the space shuttle to explode in 1986, to have memorised Pi to three hundred and twenty-two places. The chasm that exists in all of us – between who we imagine ourselves to be and the person we truly are – was to prove disastrous for him. Several times he calculated – by what means we never knew – the date for the end of the world and, when proven wrong, would lament the planet's failure to accord with his predictions. 'I don't understand it,' he would say. 'I don't get it. I guess I'll have to, you know, get my shoes fixed for winter after all, eh?'

Then a nurse would enter and give him some pills which he'd swallow without demur, without fear, like a child. From outside, on the wet lawn, I could hear the chatter of other patients and their relatives, the occasional hoot of wild laughter.

One of these nights by the sports field, I heard a tinkling of tiny bells. Someone in one of the nearby houses must have had one of those wind chimes hanging from a tree.

I sensed, rather than saw, my father look up. 'I think you should go home now,' he said after a long pause.

Now comes the hardest part, the least believable part, which is why the official police incident report ends here.

When I was about ten I asked my mother what had happened to my grandfather. I had, of course, heard much talk about him but I struggled to untangle the various strands and theories into anything coherent, a narrative I might be able to tell anyone.

She sighed and pulled me to her. A long silence. For a minute we listened to a pot bubble on the stove. 'Your grandfather vanished a long time ago. Your father was there and he claims he was taken by some strange . . . people one evening.' Here she paused, tearful, shaking her head. 'That's when it all began, really. Your father's problems. He wasn't like this when we were married. That started after.'

She showed me several photos stored in a box in her bedroom. My grandfather looked a lot like my father – the same slightly stooped stance, a way of looking sideways as if expecting to detect something from the tail of his eye.

'Something bad might have happened to your grandfather,' my mother went on, 'but we'll probably never know. I think he'd had enough. He had a few problems of his own. It's very sad.' No sign of him, she said, was ever found.

'Maybe someone *did* take him?' I said. 'Like gangsters or something.'

She looked at me long and hard. 'I think that's unlikely. You know that part of the creek down behind the oval? He fell in there and drowned. He was quite old.'

'Why didn't they find him, then?'

She paused. 'Sometimes people aren't found when they drown. They get washed away and are lost forever.'

Even in mid-winter that part of the creek was so shallow that it was difficult to imagine anyone drowning in there, let alone being washed away. My mother knew that as well as I did, but I decided against contradicting her. She must have divined my scepticism, however, because she held me out at arm's length to regard me, as she did when she was trying to be serious and treat me like an adult. 'So stay away from there, okay.'

I nodded.

'Do you promise?'

'Yes.'

My father stood and peered out over the sports field, which had by now become almost totally subsumed in darkness. He gave a short cry, strangely triumphant. 'At long last,' he said, and skidded down the dewy incline. He paused at the bottom and turned to face me. 'You should go home now,' he said again.

I was terrified of leaving him there alone. Even then I probably had an inkling of what was going to happen. I shook my head.

'Are you quite sure?' he asked.

'Yes.'

'There might be no turning back.'

I nodded.

My father was torn. He looked over his shoulder into the darkness, then back to me. He held out one hand. A strange expression took hold of his features. 'Then would you mind holding my hand? I am afraid.'

Hand in hand we walked across the field towards the creek on the far side. I sensed an urgency in my father, but we walked slowly and deliberately, as if he were keen to prolong the moment for as long as possible. We didn't speak. Our shoes squelched through the mud in the centre of the field. Although there was no wind to speak of, I heard more clearly and more often the tinkling of the wind chime I had detected earlier.

He squeezed my hand. 'I love you, my son, but I can't resist any longer. I don't really want you to see what I am about to show you, but I don't want you to think that I was merely mad.'

I squeezed back to let him know that I knew he loved me and that I also knew he had done his best, but couldn't stay with us. This was not really knowledge but, rather, something more profound, like instinct, encoded in my very DNA.

'Will you be able to find your way home by yourself?' he asked.

'Yes.'

At the far end of the field, beyond a tattered wire fence, the ground sloped down steeply and the grass gave way to a mess of blackberry and thistle. A vague track carved by dog-walkers and neighbourhood children over the years led through these bushes to the dirty creek at the bottom. There were no houses on this side of the field.

And there we paused, my father and I, hand in hand for the final time. My heart hammered in my breast.

Despite his flaws, perhaps even because of them, I loved my father deeply. He was wayward, but exceedingly kind. Even when I was a child he always treated me with great courtesy, as if I were a small monarch from a foreign land. To every question great and trivial he addressed himself with equal gravity. He explained as best he could the laws of physics to his children and drew detailed diagrams of the solar system. He told us of the songlines, of Leichhardt, of the offside rule. He made me a pinhole camera and came up with a plausible explanation as to why Peter Rabbit wore a cardigan but no trousers. My father was not all conspiracies and madness, and in that moment, when we waited at the edge of the bushland, all my love for him coalesced in what

I can only describe as a warm ball of feeling high in my boyish chest.

After several minutes I became aware – by what precise means I couldn't say – that we were being observed. There was a twitch in the bushes, followed by an intimation of snuffling. Again the sound of small bells. My father breathed heavily. His hand was warm and dry. I made out smudges of light coming along the path. I gasped and my father gave a simultaneous cry, not of shock, but of recognition – as if a problem that had long vexed him were suddenly solved.

Later, I told the police he left me on the low hill and vanished into the darkness.

'It was dark by then?' the nice policewoman asked.
'Yes.'
'And you didn't see where he went?'
'No.'
'Did you see any other people?'
'No.'
'Are you quite sure?'
'No. Yes, I mean. I'm sure.'

And then he let go of my hand and he was gone, those last words lingering on the night air, and I remembered what he'd told me once about the problem of admitting the possibility of one extraordinary thing, that it meant you must admit the possibility of them all.

The Age of Terror

I AM NO stranger to the middle of the night, to its creaks and whispers. It is the time when one is most clearly able to see into the core of oneself, a moment I relished when I was a younger and vainer woman but which I now find almost unendurable. And yet, despite a regularity that grows with each passing year, I am still always surprised to find myself lying on my bed at ungodly hours, staring into the darkness. Should I live another ten years, I can imagine spending entire nights awake. Perhaps this unprovoked waking is no surprise; after all, night is where memory resides and, as a bear lives off its fat during long, cold winters, the elderly are sustained by their memories.

The first thing I do, as my eyes adjust to the gloom, is listen for Graham's breathing. He will be eighty-two next birthday and his health is, as they say, failing. Even now his breath catches like a bicycle chain slipping a cog. But at least he is still alive, thank God. I dread the day – or the night, more likely — when I shall have to put a finger to the artery at his neck, the way I once saw someone do a long time ago. I don't even really know what to feel for. A mild throb, I suppose. A pulse. All I recall is the expression on the ambulance officer's face. It struck me at the time how similar he looked to a trout fisherman feeling for tremble on his line.

Of course, the night also offers the time and space to imagine the things one would still like to do. It is as if a lifetime of regrets, having accreted about my joints and the ventricles of my heart while sleeping, are dislodged and make themselves known: read that damn Proust epic everyone is supposed to read; sail the Mediterranean; learn an instrument. Naturally, there are other, more profound, regrets: affairs never pursued; opportunities squandered. Once, forty years ago, a gentlemanly artist cornered me at one of those inner-city parties populated by the absurdly tasteful and made me an offer I could — and did — refuse but have pondered ever since. Every now and then I hear of him when I have almost forgotten his face and, when I do, it never fails to inspire in me a mild shiver of longing. Not that I regret my time with Graham. On the contrary, he has been my saviour in many ways; I could never have done it without him.

Sadly, the middle of the night is also the moment when one is most acutely aware that one will now never get around to accomplishing these undone things and that one must be content with one's *lot*, as it now stands. At this stage of life, the die is pretty much cast. The Italians, bless them, even have a word for it: *caducità*, the terrible chasm between our attempts to construct our lives and the slow ruin of time. In other words: *it is all too late*. Might explain why the Italians have failed to produce much since the Renaissance, aside from Fellini, of course.

Inevitably, at times like this, I think of Peter. I calculate his age had he lived. The kind of man he might have become. Not that different, most likely, from the boy he was, who was not that different from the baby he had been. He would be fifty in April. Still fifty in April, still the same age I calculated last night and the night before. When pregnant, I imagined him as an apostrophe nestled in my womb, a grammatical scratch that unfurled into a letter, then a word, a sentence and finally into a story of his very own, a tale of no small woe. I knew something was wrong from the moment he was placed, like a chunk of bloody meat, at my breast. Graham sensed it as well, although neither of us spoke of it for some months, as if to articulate our worst fears might give them breath, unleash them.

Not that it mattered. When he was six months old I would inhale his milk-damp breath on nights like this, with the light just so, and a dim, naive hope of a future. By the age of three, he seemed to have extra limbs: always clumsy, his chin always glistening with drool. When he turned five we organised a birthday party. Not one of the brats we invited from the neighbourhood showed up. God, how we persevered throughout that dry afternoon: the smattering of family, everyone mortified, striving valiantly to inject enthusiasm into the occasion, still afraid to speak of his strangeness.

I remember the sad-eyed Pole we had hired to juggle for the children took Peter's utter indifference to his coloured sticks and balls as a personal affront. I could never determine if I was more aggrieved by the lack of pain the dismal event caused Peter – another 'developmental hiccup' – or by my own realisation of the wickedness of small children and parents who would organise such a boycott. You think you know people, but they always have something hidden away. It's an awful lesson, corrosive, and one I am still glad my son was never equipped to learn.

Graham snuffles and rolls in his sleep. He clears his throat as if preparing to speak, but says nothing. It has not been uncommon, in recent years, for him to talk in his sleep, sit up, stare at me and mumble, 'Jesus, Helen, what have you done?' or 'The nursery is burning' or some such nonsense before collapsing back onto the bed. The poor thing even went through a stage of sobbing himself awake. When he first started talking in his sleep, I would tell him in the morning of his outbursts and we would laugh, sometimes uneasily. Now I rarely bother. Let the night have its secrets, is what I think. There is nothing to be gained.

The water glass on the bedside table is empty. With effort, in the manner of the old woman I have somehow become, I disentangle myself from the blankets and sit on the edge of the bed. The deflated inner tubes of my breasts dangle against my stomach, long since emptied of their uses: maternal, erotic or otherwise. Two bony knees peer like tortoises from beneath my nightie. There is no glory in ageing, but unlike life's earlier difficult periods – adolescence or youth or even middle age – one cannot, of course, wish it to end. In the en suite I gulp a glass of tap water. It is immensely satisfying and I drink again. The tiles are cool beneath my feet. I feel slightly hungry. It is 4 am so I may as well go downstairs, have a snack and struggle with yesterday's cryptic crossword for a couple of hours before the day gets underway.

The stairway is lined with artworks and framed photographs of family scenes, lost places that are recognisable even in the half-light: our wedding day, a thousand years ago, in another country; Graham as a young man in Scotland, with his mop of ginger hair that would stay with him for life; a black-and-white snap of a baby cousin in a metal washtub. And Peter on a swing in a park: the photo creamy with sunlight that seems, even now, many years later, to explode from his laughing head. There he is again, the Christmas we drove to South Australia to stay in a rented beach house minutes from the sea. The best summer we had together. The last summer. Poor Peter. Still everywhere. Perhaps it is true that we are defined not by what we possess but by what we no longer have. The press had a field day, of course. Dug out a dreadful photo of me from God knows where. Interviewed other parents. Pure hell. Even now, the sound of a newspaper thudding against the front door at dawn releases in me a flood of mild panic. *What now?*

I make a pot of tea, open the kitchen door to the garden, turn the radio on low and settle in to tackle twelve down, on which I was left stranded last night. *Sailor posted as missing.* Six letters. Radio National murmurs: a boffin talking about a creature called, believe it or not, the vampire squid, which lives in the deepest parts of the ocean. This beast apparently has the largest eyes relative to body size of any animal, but also – thanks to its body being covered in light-producing organs of some sort – the ability to turn itself 'on' and 'off' so as to see at depths where light doesn't penetrate. Quite a handy ability, I imagine, and one I could do with myself should I continue to wake throughout the night. Would cut the electricity bill, at any rate.

Although I grumble about it, there is a special pleasure to be found in the early morning. Indeed, there is something quite benthic about the ground floor of our old house at this time, a sense of existing in a time zone of one's own, far from the ordinary world. The rules might well be different here. One might almost expect to glimpse one of these vampire fish, or another bizarre creature that has evolved miles from human sight, far from anywhere, eyeless. Aside from myself, naturally.

Six letters. *Sailor*. It has rained in the night and damp garden smells drift inside. *Posted as missing*. Trees crackle and drip. *Sailor posted as missing*, six letters. '*Missing*' the definition, no doubt. Graham would probably be able to do these crosswords far faster than I will ever be able to, but he has more or less given up on them. Says he has run out of use for words. Sometimes there is only so much you can say.

I don't know how long I have been sitting here when I become aware of strange, high-pitched sounds coming from outside. At first I assume them to be an auditory hallucination but the noise, or noises, persists and I am compelled to investigate. I have to admit to feeling quite terrified, but call out nonetheless in my quavering, 79-year-old woman's voice. 'Hello?' The sounds stop for a few seconds before redoubling in vigour. They have the sibilance of a coven of tiny witches, a sound like nothing I have ever heard before and I stand there in the middle of my huge kitchen, barefoot, clad only in a nightgown, wondering what on earth has come to visit me, what creature has at last discovered my whereabouts. Old thoughts, foolish thoughts. The noises intensify again. I am stranded in the middle of the kitchen, the knives out of reach, Graham asleep upstairs, far from any refuge when I realise what it is. Kittens. Of course. Our tabby cat Sally, who has been lugging her swollen belly around for weeks, has finally given birth.

Sure enough, in her basket in the laundry she is lying on her side with her blind brood mauling at her teats. She looks drunk, exhausted, but utters a croaky meow in greeting and allows me to stroke her head. Poor thing. This is her third brood because Graham won't allow me to spay her. Her babies root about in her damp and bloody fur and clamber over each other like wingless bats. There are five of them. Every so often, Sally licks the fur at her chest before collapsing back again. I know more or less how she feels. The fatigue peculiar to having given birth arrives, like a comet, from another solar system altogether. *Depleted, drained, battered* are utterly inadequate. It needs its very own dictionary entry, its very own *dictionary*. Perhaps the Italians have a word for that as well? More likely the Indians; they pop out millions of babies. That would be one for the crossword setters. *Seven across, five letters. A Hindi word for the exhaustion of having given birth.* Wherever this word exists, in whatever language, they might also have a better one for *pain*.

I fetch Sally a fresh saucer of milk and sit with her awhile. It's starting to get light. Soon Graham will wander in and crouch down to peer happily at the new kittens and smile his smile of quiet satisfaction. Although we will give them away we will probably spend much of today bandying around possible names for the new additions based on perceived characteristics. Dopey or Killer or some such. Graham's enduring love of animals is one of the things I still adore about him, when his ten-year-old self is closest to the surface, like the imp in the bottle.

After ten minutes or so it becomes apparent that one of the kittens is struggling to get its fair share of milk. A black and white one, already smaller than the others. The runt of the litter. The four other kittens shoulder it aside every time it tries to jam its little face into Sally's fur. Not nastily, but in the way the strong, in their enthusiasm, inevitably take more than they require. The little one has a scratchy cry and makes periodic attempts to snaffle its way in, but then gives up. Sally makes no effort to help it. Like a cartoon creation the kitten flops back unsteadily on its bum and stares up at me with cloudy eyes, perhaps seeking assistance. There is a speck of what I presume to be amniotic fluid on its nose. Again it squeaks. We watch each other for some time, the kitten and I. Occasionally it stares at its brothers and sisters happily gorging away, before turning back to me. It is heartbreaking. Time passes. The little thing utters pitiful cries, almost emptied of sound. Again it attempts to join the family, only to be batted away by a rival's paw.

Eventually, I stand up and fetch one of the large ancient cushions from the cane garden chair. Outside it is light. It will be a sunny day, but cold. My favourite kind of weather. I pause a moment in the garden, inhaling the smells. You reach an age where every new day merely reminds you of one already lived and at this moment I am reminded inexplicably of a morning when I was a teenager, in the house where I grew up, having breakfast with my parents, the smell of freshly brewed tea, the way Mother placed her hand on Father's arm when they shared a joke.

Back inside I pick up the tiny kitten. It mewls against my chest, ever hopeful. Even its claws seem soft, malformed, ill equipped for a lifetime of struggle. We have a small moment, draw solace from each other, before I put the cushion on the floor in the corner, place the kitten in its middle, fold it over and lean on it with all my weight. I am sure it struggles, but I am unable to feel it. The cushion is large and doughy. Sally watches me, her ears pinned back for a few seconds before she relaxes and allows her head to fall back in the folds of the blanket lining her basket. She knows it's for the best.

It is only after some time, roused by the sounds of Graham pottering about in the kitchen, that I realise my face is wet with tears, and the cushion, doubtless damp from overnight rain, has become even wetter. Then Graham appears in the laundry doorway. He beams when he sees Sally's kittens but then turns to where I squat on the floor with the cushion beneath my knees and his expression alters slightly. We say good morning and mutter approving things about the kittens and how well our Sally has done. There is a brief lull in which the only sounds are those of Sally purring and the chirp of birds in the garden. Then Graham asks me, in his special off-hand voice, what I have got under 'there', meaning the cushion, but I can tell by his face he already knows.

Dark the Water, So Deep the Night

1

THE LITTLE PLACE was different in those days; this was before the organic grocers and the prayer flags arrived, long before the rich lesbians on their yoga-and-quinoa retreats. It was just another cold, grubby country town. My brother Robert and I would sometimes row across the lake in our little wooden boat to play on the heap of mine tailings on its far side. War games mostly, extravagant deaths, injuries, missions to capture enemy bunkers. We were two boys, motherless; violence came naturally.

One day we stumbled on a red Datsun 120Y abandoned in the forest. Like explorers at an ancient ruin, we hovered nearby for some time, silent, just watching. Then, as if on a prearranged signal, we wandered across to it. The car was trashed. Its windscreen had been stove in with rocks and the upholstery was ripped and stained. It smelled of mildew and old beer. Cigarette butts littered the ground, along with broken glass, beer cans and a pair of blue jeans as stiff as cardboard.

We began to ride in the car every day. We took turns sitting in the driver's seat with one elbow hanging out the window, trying to press the pedals – which were unyielding – and wrestling the steering wheel from side to side. We fantasised about getting away, of course, leaned back and dreamed, glancing around as if taking in the scenery as we sped by. Going for a spin, we called it.

The girl appeared late one afternoon from the forest, like a hitchhiker. Robert and I stopped what we were doing and silently watched her through the shattered windscreen, unsure, at first, if she even knew we were there. If my brother was afraid, he didn't show it. The girl wore a grubby blue t-shirt, cut-off jean shorts and, on her head, a Viking helmet with two horns. She glided towards us and hovered a few metres away, near the passenger-side window. Her face was grave and luminous, doomed, as if she had stepped from an old painting. Dark eyes, a little red mouth. She held up one hand, palm out, fingers splayed, whether in benediction, greeting or warning it was hard to tell.

'You think death is fun?' she sneered.

The lake was created when a small village in the valley was flooded some decades earlier. It was extremely deep. Apparently some people had refused to leave the town before it was submerged – like those ship's captains who remained on the deck of their sinking vessel – and I imagined them in their watery houses: sitting on their couches staring resolutely ahead, cups of tea at hand, hair floating like seaweed about their pale and swollen faces.

Various items, having drifted loose from whatever bound them to the lake's bottom, floated occasionally to its surface. Toys, bits of plastic, clothes, playing cards, scraps of paper. Once a stuffed cat, which bobbed about for several days before sinking again. Books, bones, a child's pink underpants. Lakes are very different to other bodies of water. Unlike a river, say, or an ocean, a lake is not so constantly renewed.

The lake water was almost always icy cold – even in summer. On winter mornings a ghostly layer of fog seethed across its surface. Sometimes it iced over, but the ice was never very thick and we were sternly warned away from ever attempting to walk or skate on it. Our mother used to swim across the lake and back several times a week, except in the coldest months. *I'm going away for a while,* she would announce to inform the household where she would be for the next hour or so. She liked to swim in the early evening best, and I recall her standing at the shore, snapping a swimming cap on her head before plunging in and churning across, until she grew smaller and finally disappeared in the gloom. I used to fret dreadfully when she fell from sight, so one day she handed me a pair of binoculars to observe her progress, and from then on would blow me a kiss when she reached the other side to indicate that she was fine, not to worry. Then I would wait on the shore until she trudged gleamingly from the muddy water and say, almost every time, *You never regret a swim*. As she dried herself she sometimes regaled me with what she had seen on her journey, extravagant tales populated with the spectral residents of the submerged town: of the baker setting out his wares in the window of his shop; of old Mrs Jones doing her knitting up a tree; of the local Aboriginal tribe conducting a ceremony for their boys. When I was older she asked me to join her, but half-heartedly; I have since become an avid swimmer myself and have come to recognise the pleasure in the solitude and the sense of entering another dimension, a netherworld we might visit but never fully inhabit.

Robert and I didn't talk about the strange, long-legged girl on the way back and we didn't mention her to our father, but we returned to the far side of the lake the following day, and the day after. The girl's name was Leonora Bloom. She told us she was fourteen, a couple of years older than me and a year younger than Robert. She wore the same clothes every day, including the Viking helmet. Her breath always smelled of vinegar, and her allure – if you could call it that – was slinky and unpredictable.

We sat in the Datsun and gossiped about local people. She told us she had travelled the world and had visited the casinos of Vegas, the cafes of Athens, the forests of Tasmania. I had never been anywhere, so the mere thought of such places thrilled me. I skimmed stones across the surface of the lake and imagined them tumbling through the dark water, their descent like those of feathers in air: rocking to and fro until they came to rest among the skeleton of the old town. Perceiving the world beneath the surface was a kind of curse for me; rarely did I see something than I immediately invoked its shadow.

'You should come and meet Jesus,' Leonora Bloom announced one afternoon.

Bearded, wild-eyed Jesus was an itinerant man who was spotted stalking through town every year or so. All sorts of rumours swirled about him: parties, squalor, drugs; he'd fought in the Vietnam war; he'd once killed a cop; he had twelve children. I was terrified at the thought of meeting him. About two years earlier we were driving to the grocery store and my dad pointed him out. Jesus was wearing a plaid shirt and tattered jeans; it took me several seconds to identify him among the crowd waiting for the dole office to open. 'There's our saviour, boys,' my dad chuckled, 'risen from the dead.'

'We can't go,' I whispered to Robert. 'It's getting too late.' I sounded like a scared little girl and, what's worse, I knew it.

My brother was driving. In the back seat, Leonora Bloom removed her Viking helmet, shook out her dirty blonde hair and refitted the helmet to her head. Robert watched her attentively in the cracked rear-view mirror and although no one said anything, it was obvious a decision had been made.

'Turn right here and pull over,' she said as she clambered across the seat.

We followed Leonora Bloom through the pines, her legs thin as matchsticks, glint of late sunlight on her helmet. I turned to look back across the lake and thought I saw my father standing at the lounge room window, a tiny figure, so forlorn. His name was Frank. He was melancholy, subject to insomnia, a lover of crosswords. Although I suspected he was barely aware of it himself, he was still waiting, patiently waiting, for my mother's return. At that moment I missed him terribly. A cigarette was probably burning between the fingers of his right hand. Our empty house, with its smell of sodden tea leaves and its hum of fridge.

I waved, but there was no response. I doubt he saw me. No surprise in that; children didn't really exist for the fathers of my generation. Besides, by then it was almost dark.

Our mother was long gone. We all missed her, of course, but for Robert the pain never ceased. He was angry and dejected. I feared for him. He wept almost every night. After all, he said, he had known her longer than I had. This always carried the force of rebuke, the implication being that my own grief had not been sufficiently earned. His heart felt dislocated, he said – this strange phrase accompanied by twisting his hands together, as if wringing out a sponge or breaking the neck of a small animal.

Robert told me other stories about her, things I didn't remember or was too young to have been conscious of, but which, over time and retelling, began to resemble my own memories: her fondness for Turkish delight; the time she dressed down the butcher for his overpriced beef; the powdery scent of her clothes.

Leonora Bloom led my brother and me to their camp, which was a cluster of old, broken-down mining shacks. There was no one else around. The largest building was constructed of dark weatherboard and built on the side of a hill. Its eaves were garlanded with vines. It seemed to hover above the ground, rather than sit upon it. Weirdest of all, however, was the fact that Robert and I had never encountered it before, even though it probably wasn't further than two kilometres from where we had lived our entire lives.

'How could we have never found this?' I said.

Leonora Bloom shot me a scornful glance. Her forehead gleamed with perspiration. She licked the sweat from her upper lip. 'Because only a few of us know how to get out here,' she said. 'You think we want the whole town here?'

I opened my mouth to speak but she was already walking away, with Robert trotting behind like a puppy. We sat on a big cane chair hanging from a tree by a chain, sharing a can of warm lemonade. I don't know what I had expected, but it was peaceful there, almost completely silent apart from the birds. You could dimly hear traffic from the main street, but that was all. Leonora Bloom and my brother were tickling each other and giggling. I sat on the lip of the chair looking the other way, pretending I wasn't bothered.

After a while I realised that a young woman was watching us from behind some trees. She had long hair and wore a tattered yellow dress. Then I saw an older man at the corner of the house. Another man was watching us from a dirty window. This man was bearded, hollow-faced, intense. On his head was a crown of what looked like dry, tangled vine.

*

Later, Robert rowed us home across the lake towards the orange glow of our kitchen, which was the only light to be seen on the far side. By then it was so dark and so quiet that we might have been astronauts navigating towards a distant space station. There was only the sound of our oars in the locks, their rhythmic splash. I trailed my fingers in the cool, black water. Finally, we beached the little boat, dragged it up to the grass in front of the house and flipped it over to drain. Robert went and stood by the shore, looking across the lake. I stood next to him. There was nothing to see, of course: just darkness across the expanse of gleaming water.

'We shouldn't go back there,' he said.

'Why?'

'Just don't, okay.'

'But why?'

But he was already walking away.

2

I started hanging around at the camp as often as I could. Aside from Jesus and Leonora Bloom there were two or three other adults staying there whom I saw only occasionally. I was never introduced to any of them and mostly they ignored me, like a pet occasionally underfoot. Perhaps this was why I liked the place – no one asked polite questions about school or treated me as if I were made of glass on account of what had happened to my mother; probably they knew nothing about her. Robert never joined me and although I sensed his disapproval, he did nothing to stop me going over there and he never told our dad.

Jesus had tattoos the size of insects on his hands and forearms. Numbers, a swastika, little dots and, along the flesh of his inner arm, a list of women's names in cursive script, like signatures. *Alice, Marilyn, Lorraine.*

'Innocence is the great lie of childhood,' he said to me once. 'Children are equally capable of evil. Maybe more so.'

He said these sort of things often and afterwards I would lie in bed at home pondering his words as our father drifted through the house – smoking, drinking cups of tea, running a hand through his hair.

Alice. My mother's name.

Our house was cold. Any sunlight through its windows was thin. Blankets on our knees in front of the radiator, toast and baked beans for dinner, watching TV through the night and, in the morning, the honk of ducks across the water.

Sometimes at night I listened to an ancient transistor radio, scrolling through the stations with it pressed to my ear. I had by this time constructed an elaborate fantasy in which my mother had run away to join some sort of underground political resistance. I knew it was ridiculous, but I still hoped to hear her voice on the radio. I never did, of course. There was only music, lots of static, old tunes, news of the world.

When my mother disappeared, my father entered a strange state that he was yet to wake from. Sometimes I watched him sleeping, which he did with a look of intense concentration on his face. Grey hair at his temples and a pockmark on the bridge of his nose from childhood chicken pox. I hovered over him, inhaling his bitter, diazepam-stained breath, hoping to detect something of his dreams. I assumed his dreams were similar to mine: my mother walking by the lake in her blue dress with its pattern of white flowers, my mother's expression of bemused happiness, scratching her calf with the toe of her other foot. Once, when I was leaning over him, his eyes flicked open and, momentarily startled, he said, 'Oh, it's only you,' before rolling over and going back to sleep.

Several times, prompted by I don't know what, there would be a party at the house on the other side of the lake and the residents dressed up and there was an abundance of food and wine. How to describe those nights? The fires, the feasts, dancing, the complete relinquishing of the senses? Women with antlers, men in cloaks. Snouts glistening with juices, candlelight and smoke, the sharp fizz of cider. It was strange and glorious, not of this world. It was ramshackle, heavenly, sublime. Yes, they took me in.

When it became cold, Jesus wore a fur coat so bulky that, combined with his large beard and long hair, he resembled a shaggy bear lumbering around the house. 'So,' he said to me late one afternoon as we sat together at a chipped wooden table in the kitchen, 'do you think you can tell heaven from hell?'

I didn't say anything; I was never sure, when he spoke like this, if I was actually supposed to answer, or merely listen. I smirked a little, trying to give the impression that I understood his cryptic comments only too well but didn't, at that precise moment, feel the urge to respond. I was drawn to him, like fire; but, like fire, he frightened me. I could hear music coming from somewhere in the depths of the house. The sound was muddy. Then a woman's sudden laughter, like glass shattering. I longed for someone to appear, distract him and allow me to slide away unnoticed.

He waved a hand around. 'This is not all there is, you know. No. Entire worlds, whole *galaxies*. If you could see what I have seen, my son. Attack ships off the shores of Orion. Vast, hidden cities. The march of soldiers. Things. Such . . . things. You think events happen for a reason, don't you?'

I shrugged; I didn't really know what I believed.

'That the world is some sort of vending machine, meting out experiences. That if you are good and put the correct change in the slot, then good will come to you – if not in this life, then in the next. Isn't that right?'

I did more or less believe this but it seemed a childish thing to admit, like confessing to a belief in Santa Claus or fairies or God.

'But sometimes things just happen. The world doesn't care. The universe doesn't care. The wind blows, trees fall over. People's hearts stop working. Meteors strike the earth, waves crash upon the shore. We tell stories to impose order on the world, to give things meaning. To give us hope.' He lapsed into silence, as if overwhelmed.

'Why do they call you Jesus?' I ventured at last.

His gaze, which had lost focus during his little soliloquy, turned on me. 'Did your family never take you to church?'

I shook my head. My dad hardly took us anywhere, not even to school.

For a long time Jesus inspected the tattoos scattered across the backs of his hands, which he often did when he was thinking. Then he looked at me with his clear, blue eyes and, although he said nothing for some time, I understood at that moment why they all adored him; his smile was so unguarded, frailer than butterfly wings.

'Because they murdered me,' he said at last, 'but I returned.'

3

One afternoon I encountered Leonora Bloom squatting on a tree stump by the lake shore, fishing. On the bank beside her was a little smoking fire of twigs. There was a knife in her plastic bucket, but no fish. Inedible, thick-bodied serpents lived in the lake and occasionally loomed beneath the surface like half-remembered dreams, peering up before disappearing again into the depths. They resembled the detached forearms of very muscular men. I never knew what they were called; we called them lake slugs. They had silvery scales and small, very sharp teeth, although they were harmless to humans. Once Robert and I hauled one from the lake in a net and watched it gasp and writhe about on the muddy bank until it died: appalled by its death, too appalled to shove it back into the water.

I opened my mouth to tell Leonora Bloom about these creatures but something in her manner made me hold my tongue. The fire softly crackled. She dragged in her line, replaced the bait and flung it expertly back into the water. She seemed annoyed at my disturbing her, but it felt awkward to leave without saying anything, so I tossed a few twigs into the fire and asked her why she always wore her helmet.

She rolled her eyes. 'Because I'm a fucking Viking. What do you reckon?'

A tiny glint of sunlight caught my eye on the far side of the lake. I glanced at our house. 'That's probably my dad,' I said, gesturing lamely, 'watching us through his binoculars.'

Leonora Bloom followed my gaze, her features arranged in a sceptical scowl, before turning back to her line. 'I had an imaginary family when I was a kid, too,' she muttered as she threaded a worm onto her hook. 'It was very comforting.'

I felt, suddenly, like weeping and stood up to go but, perhaps wishing to make amends, Leonora Bloom asked me to pass her the knife from the bucket. When I'd done so, she cut her line with it and fiddled about, replacing the hook she had been using with a smaller one. Then she cast again while I stood by, wanting to leave while not wishing to reveal my hurt. From the house behind the trees drifted a deep rumble of Jesus's laughter.

'Is he your dad?' I asked.

'*No!*' she scoffed, as if the question were one of the stupidest she'd heard in her life. 'He's just some guy. No. A saint, really. That's what he is. Guy's a fucking saint.'

'He said he had been murdered.'

'Don't you believe in miracles?'

Unsure how else to respond, I shrugged. I didn't really believe in those things, but I sensed that this answer would only invite further scorn. I could already tell that she despised me; usually it took people longer.

'It's true,' she continued. 'A man killed him in jail. You should see the massive scar on his chest. And now he can do all sorts of things. Walk on water. See the future.'

'Where are your parents, then?'

She pulled in her line and began packing up her fishing gear. 'They died ages ago in an accident. Your mother's dead, too, isn't she?'

No one had ever actually said this to me before, but in that moment I recognised the truth of it. And, after the shock, it was a relief, an infection finally eased. Of course. Of course she was dead.

I nodded. 'But they've never . . . found her. There was never a funeral or anything.'

'That's tough. Funerals are important. You know, we believe that when people are born, an old woman sitting under a tree carves into a stick a bunch of notches that indicate how many years the person will live for. Fifty, twenty-five, whatever. It's all fixed,' she added. 'It's fate. There's nothing you can do.' She paused, to ensure that I had understood her meaning. 'You think she made it into heaven?'

It was an absurd question, but one I had considered many times myself. Robert and I had even discussed it years ago, before he clammed up completely. In my imagination, my mother's afterlife was somehow tied up with the lake – not necessarily that the lake was the site of her death, but was her resting place, her hereafter. Of all of us, she had enjoyed the water the most and it was mainly due to her love of the lake that my father moved here when my brother was born. But I didn't answer Leonora Bloom.

'We used to place our dead in boats that would then be set on fire.' She waved one hand out over the lake. 'A burning boat drifting on the river in heavy fog. Imagine that.'

By *we* I gathered she meant the Vikings. I stared over the lake and out there, with late sunlight smashing off its surface, it was not hard to conjure such a scene. Yes. The flames gnawing on the timber, smoke, the craft sizzling as it capsized into the water. 'But why did they burn everything?'

She seemed annoyed at such a prosaic query. 'It helps the person get to heaven, of course. To the halls of Valhalla. You put all their really valuable stuff in it with them. You know, their swords and axes and armour and stuff. It's a mark of respect. Eases the way. Maybe it's also good for the relatives to get rid of all their stuff. All the reminders of them, I guess.' She stared at me for a long while. 'He was right about you. It's almost like . . . I don't know, like you have too much blood in you. You know, this is a . . . nasty little town. There are much better places. You should come with us when we move on.'

'Go with you? Really?'

'Sure. But you'd have to pass our test first. Like an initiation.'

'What would I have to do?'

'We can't tell you unless you agree to it first.'

'That's stupid.'

'Well. That's the law. Our law.'

'Is it hard?'

'The test? Of course it's hard. Otherwise it wouldn't be a test, would it?'

I was excited by the invitation, off-hand as it was, and although I understood she wouldn't divulge anything further about this initiation, I didn't want the conversation to end yet; it was a rare moment of intimacy. 'Where are you going anyway? After here, I mean.'

She stood up and turned to go, then hesitated. With a throw of her chin she indicated our house on the other side of the lake. 'You still got some of your mother's things over there? Like clothes and stuff. Jewellery? Anything like that?'

I nodded.

'Cos we could do the burning boat thing with just her things, you know. As long as there's a photo of the person. That's still pretty useful. Why don't you bring her stuff over here tomorrow.'

I immediately saw the rightness of this proposal, without question, as if an ill-shaped peg had finally, after many attempts, found its very own ill-shaped slot.

'Is there anything 'specially valuable,' she went on, 'like rings or anything? Necklaces? Gold, of course. Anything made of gold is really good.'

But all I could manage to do was nod, for by this time I was crying so hard I was unable to speak.

Even in my half-sleep I knew that my father had entered my room, so when I opened my eyes, it was no surprise to find him sitting there in the darkness. He was sitting on my desk chair, which was much too small for him, so that he was hunched over, his body a tight little knot. A cigarette burned between the fingers of one hand and when he raised it to inhale, momentarily illuminating his features, he resembled a monster from a story book: frightening, pitiful, misunderstood. I could make out his beaky nose, his bruised eyes, the gleam of his high forehead and the silver streak in his fringe.

I remained silent, as if sleeping, but I longed to tell him something to relieve his anguish – but what? That I loved him? That Alice would be coming back, that she wouldn't? That I was here – right here! – only a metre away from him, breathing in and out? Alive. How was a family supposed to be? Were they all like ours, bound by such darkness? In town I had observed other people's families, fascinated at how they interacted, and it seemed so distant from my own experience that I might have been watching through my father's binoculars; indeed, my own family members were like wild animals each living in their own habitats, occasionally crossing paths before slinking further away into the bush, as if ashamed of each other.

Idly, he picked up a piece of Lego from my desk and stared at it intently. My father took great interest in the world and could often be found inspecting an insect or flower in the garden, totally absorbed and yet alert to anyone's approach, whereupon he might launch into an enthusiastic little speech: *Fascinating, the way the bee moves. There. See that. You know they have a complicated social system whereby* . . . And so, although very late, I half expected him to embark on a disquisition on the history of Lego as he sat at my desk turning over a little red brick in his hand. But he said nothing and I must have fallen asleep, for then it was morning.

We have come to a point in history, my father used to say, where expertise is no longer of the slightest use to us. Imagination is really what we need.

4

After school I went into my father's bedroom and sat on the end of the bed. My brother was elsewhere. My father was at work. It was silent. Spooky and comforting. The bedsheets were very cold.

I thought about the counsellor I'd seen at school a few years ago, called Susan, who talked about closure and things like that. There had been nothing to mark my mother's departure, and this was something Susan occasionally returned to over the course of our sessions; in fact, she had suggested our family perform some little ritual as a way of honouring her memory and hoping for the best. Like a prayer, I guess. I was noncommittal but said I would bring it up with my father and brother, although I never did; prayer, after all, is a kind of coal one hopes to coax into flame, but our coals had long ago turned to dust. In any case, we were unaccustomed to asking anyone, let alone God, for anything. Susan was pretty and I liked spending time with her, but I was never sure if I understood what she was talking about. She told me that things might make sense when I was older. Once, I asked her where she thought my mother might be and she sort of sagged in her seat before clearing her throat and straightening up. 'Hmm. Where do *you* think she might be?'

Our mother disappeared when I was four years old and my recollections of her had faded almost to the point of invisibility, like the tiny spot on the TV screen that glowed long after it was turned off. At the edge of memory, I sometimes glimpsed a cigarette held out glamorously to the side of her mouth; cracked lips; I occasionally detected the bitter perfume of her hairspray. This was wishful thinking, of course. Police divers had dragged the lake, photos of her were stapled to lampposts, bulletins issued. Nothing. My father was initially a suspect – as husbands invariably are – and was still regarded with great suspicion among sections of the town.

We assumed she was dead or had run off with another man, that she was living in New Zealand or had simply walked into the forest until she collapsed – each of which seemed equally possible. After all, your parents have vast lives that you know nothing about, don't they? At night, when you're asleep, they might transform into lions or mermaids; perhaps they met travellers under the stars to exchange antique manuscripts? In any case our story was hardly unique; people disappeared all the time.

Some of my mother's things were left as they were when she disappeared. Most of her clothes had been thrown out or given to charity, but a few items remained in the wardrobe. Dresses, blouses, several pairs of shoes. My mother took pride in her appearance; my parents' bedroom still possessed the vague, chalky scent of her old cosmetics. Eyeliner, tweezers, a hair clip, each item furred with dust.

From the wardrobe I gathered her dresses and shoes and shoved them into a cardboard box. On the bedside table was a framed black-and-white photo of my mother taken in Paris in the late 1950s. I placed that in the box, too. Among the bits and pieces on the dresser was a jewellery box containing a pearl necklace she was wearing in the photograph, along with three rings that had belonged to her. I sorted through them. I chose carefully. Gold was best, the girl had said.

Hurrying now, as I feared my brother or father would return home at any minute and try to stop me, I put the box of my mother's things into the bottom of the rowboat and set off for the other side of the lake.

Leonora Bloom must have seen me coming across because she was waiting for me on the far shore. She helped me beach the little boat and began rummaging through the box of my mother's possessions, holding up clothes for inspection and tipping the jewellery out onto her palm. She rubbed the pearls of the necklace against her teeth, grunted with approval and put them back into the jewellery box.

'This is pretty good. You've done well.'

I felt myself blush with pleasure. 'There's this, too. For the fire.' I lifted a small, red can of kerosene from the boat and plonked it on the muddy beach.

Leonora Bloom approached me, placed a hand on each of my shoulders and looked down into my face. Her helmet was dented and one of the horns was askew but, rather than diminish her authority, it only served, in my eyes, to heighten it; in that moment she resembled a warrior, a goddess, a saviour. I believed in her utterly. She smiled at me so warmly that I feared I might cry again.

'Leave these things with me,' she said. 'But come back tomorrow with the boat and we'll do the ritual.'

'But why not today? Now?'

She glanced over her shoulder. 'Today is not quite right. Come back tomorrow. Five o'clock. But not before then. I'll have to get everything ready. Okay? Okay?'

Eventually I nodded. With her hands still upon my shoulders, she spun me around, steered me back to the boat, waited until I had climbed back in, and shoved me off. With my back to home as I rowed, I watched her grow smaller and less distinct. Then, when I was halfway across the lake she waved – almost wistfully, it seemed – turned and disappeared into the arboreal shadows with the box of my mother's things.

5

Of course, Leonora Bloom wasn't waiting for me when I returned the following day and although I knew searching would be fruitless, I nonetheless went through the demoralising little pantomime of making my way past the abandoned Datsun to the ramshackle settlement where she and Jesus and the others had been staying. There was no trace of anyone, merely signs they had once been there: empty soft-drink cans, old mattresses, cold ashes, a busted sandshoe. The cabins were empty of people and had acquired a sinister air of abandonment. I was relieved to scramble back to my boat by the lake. A light came on in my house on the opposite shore. My father was probably frying sausages and idly wondering where I was while my brother was lying stomach-down on his bed reading *Asterix*. In that moment, they seemed so far away they might have been mere memories.

   I climbed into the moored boat and, with no one around to comfort or chastise me, I wept freely and for so long that when I was returned to myself it was almost dark. I felt hollowed out, as if my unshed tears had been my only sustenance. The trees and bushes on the other side of the lake had become indistinct. Insects fluttered about my face and frogs creaked in the nearby reeds. All those tears, I thought when I had finished. All my beautiful tears.

   I was preparing to shove the boat back into the water and row homeward when something in the gloom caught my eye. It was the cardboard box in which I'd carried my mother's stuff across. It was on its side beneath a pine tree. There were a few things still inside it. A green dress, a pair of red shoes and the photo of her in Paris, now crumpled and loose from its metal frame. Next to the battered box was the red canister of kerosene. It sloshed when I picked it up. Still full. At least they hadn't taken that.

6

I found a lighter jammed down the back of one of the old couches at the camp site and scattered the few remaining items of my mother's in the boat. Then I shook kerosene over it all. The smell was exciting, so strong and sweet and full of possibilities. I tossed my mother's photo into the boat and then stood there for a long time, my face damp with tears and my jeans splashed with kerosene, before flicking the lighter's wheel and setting its yellow spark to the fuel, which immediately exploded into flames.

The fire took hold of the boat and it wasn't long before it had darted maniacally through the bushes and trees, growing larger, hemming me in against the shore until I was forced to retreat into the lake shallows for safety. Trees crackled and popped, bushes bloomed with fire and heat. I flinched, became disoriented, then slipped on the slimy rocks by the shore and fell into the water. Soon my toes couldn't touch the bottom. My mouth filled with muddy water and I flailed and cried out but soon grew tired and it was with strange relief that I began to fall beneath the waters, as if I were being gradually drawn earthwards from a great height.

Overhead, flames shimmered on the lake's surface, across that vast and blazing firmament, and soon I was floating among fish who eyed me curiously, this stranger in their realm, drawing right up to my face before flickering away. There were yabbies and eels suspended in the green and aqueous air, bits of plastic and paper, Coke cans, a figurine of a soldier on his knees firing a rifle. I drifted through the ruins of the old town, over its tiled roofs, the very tops of skeletal trees and old poles. I was no longer afraid. And it was then that I saw, or remembered seeing, my mother, walking dreamily, swinging her arms, her hair untidy as it almost always was. She looks more beautiful and more relaxed than I recall seeing before. I call out and try to reach her but any progress is difficult. There's the current, the breeze. Finally she notices me, but her expression is not of gladness, as I might have hoped and expected but, rather, a sort of awkwardness, as if I had disturbed a private reverie. I hesitate, but eventually she smiles gamely. I wave and make to approach but sense my presence is not entirely welcome. Then my mother blows me a kiss, turns and continues serenely on her way. Soon she disappears. I am confused and dismayed. Around me the world is swirling. Dark the water, so deep the night. Bubbles and drift, the flavours of rust and mud in my mouth. I float aimlessly through the submerged town, past the bakery, a wheelbarrow, a bike on its side next to the bank. I see Mrs Jones in a tree, a girl playing with her doll, an elderly man wiping his nose. But then I sense my father's hand in my own, his arm about my waist, and although I am unsure if we are swimming

Dark the Water, So Deep the Night

or flying, he drags me from that haunted town, its steeples and trees barely visible through the thick water, until I was borne, out of the flames, across the water, towards our home on that distant shore.

Where There's Smoke

Incredible what you find without even looking. When I was about nine years old, I was kicking a football around in the back garden late in the afternoon. I was alone, as usual – or thought I was – and the day was nearly over. It was late autumn. The air was still blue and smoky from the piles of burning leaves in the neighbourhood gutters. Shooting for goal from an impossible angle, I watched my football bounce into a tangle of bushes beside the high wooden fence that bordered our neighbour's house, and when I crawled in to retrieve it I discovered a woman crouching there, damp leaves stuck to her hair like a crown. She clutched her knees, which were bare and knobbly where her dress had ridden up. I was too stunned to say a word.

'You must be Tom,' she said.

I nodded. My scuffed football was on the ground behind her. 'How did you know?' I said when at last I found my voice.

She glanced up at the old house, at the lit lounge room window, warm as a lozenge in the gloom. Soon one of my sisters would draw the curtains and the house would be absorbed into the falling night, safe and sound against the cold and dark. Realising I was clearly not the sort of child to run screaming and tell everyone about finding a stranger in his backyard, she took a few seconds to adjust her position, which must have been quite uncomfortable. 'Oh, I know *lots* of interesting things about you.'

I heard Mrs Thomson singing to herself in her kitchen next door, the *chink* of cutlery being taken from a drawer. Having stopped running around, I was getting cold, and a graze on my elbow, from when I had fallen over on the bricks, began to sting.

'I know that you love football,' the woman went on, looking around as if assembling the information from the nearby air. '*Aaaaand* that you love *Star Wars*, that you've got lots of *Star Wars* toys and things. Little figurines, I guess you'd call them.'

This was true. I'd seen *Star Wars* four times, once with my dad and then with my friend Shaun and then twice at other kids' birthday parties. In addition, I had a book of *Star Wars*, a model of an X-wing fighter, comics and several posters on my wall. The distant planet of Tatooine – with its twin suns, where Luke Skywalker had grown up – was more real to me than Darwin or the Amazon River.

I inspected the stranger more closely. She was pretty, with long hair, and freckles across her nose. She wasn't as old as my mum, but maybe a bit older than my teacher at school, Miss Dillinger. It didn't seem right that this woman was sneaking about in our garden and I was preparing to say something to that effect when she leaned forward, whispering, her red mouth suddenly so close I felt her breath on my ear. 'I *also* know that it was you who broke Mr Anderson's window last month.'

A chill seeped through me. Several weeks ago, Shaun and I were hitting a tennis ball around in his grassy garden when we discovered a much more interesting game: by employing the tennis racquets we could launch small, unripe lemons vast distances. Ones the size of golf balls were the best and, if struck correctly, would travel across several houses – maybe even as far as a kilometre, or so we imagined. With no one around we amused ourselves in this fashion until the predictable happened and we heard the smash of a distant window, followed by furious shouting that went on for several minutes. Terrified, only then cognisant of the possible outcomes of our game, we stashed the tennis racquets back in the shed, cleaned up the lemons and scurried inside to watch television and listen out for sirens or the blunt knock of a policeman at the front door. We heard later that the police were indeed summoned, but no one thought to question us about the damage because it happened so far from our houses and who would have dreamed we could throw lemons so far? Nothing was ever proven and he vehemently denied any involvement, but blame was sheeted home to an older kid called Glen Taylor, who lived closer to the Andersons and was known to be a troublemaker. This apparent escape didn't stop me from dwelling on our crime most days, however, and even now, weeks later, the sight of a police car filled me with dread, with terrifying visions of handcuffs and juvenile detention.

The stranger sat back on her haunches, evidently satisfied that alerting me to her knowledge of the incident had fulfilled its function, whatever that was. I felt the shameful heat of incipient tears. 'Are you the police?'

'Hardly.'

'Then who are you?'

She coughed once into her fist and looked around again, as if she were unsure herself. 'Don't cry,' she said at last. 'It's all right, I won't hurt you. My name is . . . Anne.'

I wiped my nose. 'But what are you doing hiding in our garden?'

A fresh pause, another glance towards my house. 'I'm not *hiding*, thank you very much. I'm always here.'

'What do you mean?'

'I'm waiting for my turn on the throne.' The woman looked at me again, and it seemed to me her mouth had tightened. 'Princess Anne, waiting to enter the castle as queen at last.'

By now it was almost dark. The woman's dress was indistinguishable from the foliage surrounding us, so that only her pale face was visible, the deep pools of her eyes; an apparition in her undersea grotto. She jumped when my mother called out for me to come inside for dinner – looked set to run off, in fact – before relaxing again at the sound of retreating footsteps and the screen door slapping shut. 'Yell out you're coming,' she whispered.

Succumbing to the innate authority adults wield over children, I did as I was told.

'Smells delicious,' she said a few seconds later. 'Like lamb.'
I nodded.

'I hear your mother is a *good little cook*.'

I was suffused with filial pride. 'She is. She makes a beautiful apple crumble, too.'

'Keeps a nice house. Tucks you in, reads you stories, makes *biscuits*.'

My mum didn't make biscuits. The curious woman didn't even seem to be addressing me but, rather, talking out loud to herself. 'That's very nice,' she continued, as if I had agreed with her summation of my mother's housekeeping capabilities. 'Why don't you bring me back some of that lamb later. Wrap a few slices in some wax paper or something. Let me try this famous lamb.'

'I don't know –'

'Go on, be a sport. And one of your father's cigarettes.'

'He gave up.'

The woman sniggered. 'Like hell he did. Why don't you look in his study. There's a green volume of Dickens on the top shelf of his bookcase, *Great Expectations*, naturally. It's hollowed out and there's a packet of Marlboros hidden in there. Bring me a couple. But don't forget the matches.'

I didn't ask how she knew this; I had a feeling I didn't want to know. I had become unaccountably afraid in the past minute or so and stood up to leave as best I could beneath the low branches. At school they advised us not to talk to strangers in the street or at the park, but no one said anything about finding one in your own garden.

'I suppose you want your ball.'

'Yes, please.'

She slung me the football. 'Nice manners. Don't forget to bring me those cigarettes after dinner. I'll be right here.'

'Okay.'

'Don't smoke them all yourself, will you, now you know where they're hidden? They're for grown-ups.'

'I don't smoke.'

'Good boy. It was nice meeting you at last, Tom. You can't tell anyone you saw me, though. Remember what I know about you and those lemons. A certain broken *window*. Don't want your mum to find out, do you? Or the police. Tell anyone you saw me here and I'll blow your whole house down. Like what's-her-name, Princess Leia.'

I didn't bother to correct her version of who Princess Leia was or what she might be capable of, and went inside for dinner. Afterwards, when everyone was watching TV, I went into my dad's study and found the cigarettes exactly where she said they would be. I stood there a long time, staring at them, before lifting the packet out of the miniature grave carved into the book. The smell of dry tobacco was both familiar and exotic, full of dark promise. On our wall calendar in the kitchen were marked the months since my father had smoked his last cigarette and the money his hard-won abstinence was saving our family. The ways of adults were as mysterious to me as a forest; they spoke often in their own unintelligible tongue. In the other room my family laughed at *M*A*S*H*, even though they were all repeats.

Without really knowing what I was doing – much less why – I withdrew a cigarette from the packet, put it between my lips and lit it. The flavour was strong and terrible. Smoke wafted into my eyes. My immediate coughing fit brought my two older sisters running to the study doorway, where they stood giggling with disbelief after calling out for our mum.

When she arrived, my mother slapped the cigarette away and demanded to know what the hell I was doing. My father was the last to arrive on the scene and he weathered my mother's tirade with his gaze fixed not on the book, with its cigarette packet-shaped hole, that my mother brandished at him as evidence of his flagrant dishonesty, but on the curtained window, as if expecting to see something unwelcome step in from outside.

Season of Hope

Mr F was short and squat, well dressed, with the sort of small, dry hands you might expect of a bureaucrat. I was horrified to observe a tiny spot of tomato sauce on his striped tie. At least I hoped it was tomato sauce. He entered the hotel room quickly, before the door was even fully open, slipping inside with more agility than I'd expect of someone of his age and build. What we were doing was highly illegal; the appointment had been complicated to organise and arranged through an intermediary. I'd never met anyone like him before – anyone who did what he did, I mean – and I was anxious. Besides that, I didn't even know his real name, so, without thinking, I stuck out my hand and said, 'You must be the abortionist.'

I heard Juliet's swift intake of breath behind me.

Mr F closed the door carefully, put down his bag, pulled the yellow curtains and turned to me with a sour little smile. Juliet sat on the end of the bed and rested one hand on her stomach before quickly removing it, as if scalded.

Then Mr F turned to me with an expression of great forbearance. 'Why don't you go and get yourself a drink or something? Some chips, perhaps? We won't be too long.'

Strangely, neither of them uttered a word when I put on my coat. I kissed the top of Juliet's head and told them I'd return in an hour.

I'd met Juliet about four months earlier at a party in Dalston. She was dancing by herself to an ancient techno song in a dingy hallway. As people arrived, they watched her enviously or indulgently for a moment, then sidled past, towards the music and dope smoke at the back. My friend Donald introduced us. She was dark-haired, scrawny and not very attractive but her Bristol accent really did something for me. She shook my hand and said, *Awright?*

I ran into her on the street late one afternoon a week later. We exchanged awkward hellos. She looked better in sunlight, but fragile, like her legs might give way at any moment. She was wearing a dark overcoat and, beneath it, a cream-coloured dress patterned with red flowers. We chatted about the weather, exchanged some gossip about mutual friends. Her eyes were blue and her voice husky. There are times in life when you'd do almost anything to get into a girl's pants, so when she asked me if I wanted to see where Nick Cave had been murdered, I shrugged and told her to lead the way.

To be honest, I only dimly remembered Cave, but Juliet knew his tale well — a long night on the booze, a misunderstanding, a hammer within reach. Violent death was so common in those long years that such events passed almost without remark. The woman who'd killed him, Juliet said, was in a psych ward somewhere. She told me you could still see the bloodstains on the carpet through the window of the flat, as if this were explanation enough for our curious pilgrimage.

We walked in silence for a while. I was acutely aware of the *tap tap tap* of her heels on the cracked footpath. The afternoon was hot and a greasy slab of pollution hovered over our heads. We passed a roadside stall selling computers, another selling fruit. Donald had told me Juliet had been to Paris before the war, so I asked her about it.

'Oh,' she said with obvious fondness, 'it was so great.'

'Is it true what they say about the Eiffel Tower?'

She stopped to light a cigarette and tossed away the match. Then she considered me, like she was debating whether I was worth entrusting with a secret. 'Yeah. It *was* beautiful. And Notre Dame. I can't believe what those fuckers did to that city. Although the Eiffel Tower was only supposed to be temporary,' she added, as if this exonerated those who had destroyed it.

She continued walking, but paused at the top of some concrete stairs. 'We'll go down here,' she explained when I caught up with her, 'and walk along the canal to Islington. That way we'll avoid the checkpoints.'

The canal smelled muddy. An oily slick coated the Coke-dark water, full of rubbish. We passed an elderly man fishing from a small rowboat on the canal, although I found it hard to imagine anything living in that water; all I'd ever seen were bicycle wheels, dozens of empty bottles and cartons and numerous deflated soccer balls. Weeds sprouted through cracks in the path beside the water.

Eventually, we sat on an old wooden bench by the canal. It was strangely peaceful and I'll always remember her lovely knees, the crease along the side of one of her burgundy Mary Janes, the way she fidgeted with her cigarette. A bird hopped about on the grassy bank in front of us and I wondered if normal life was like this: sitting by a canal on a mild afternoon with a pretty girl, smoking cigarettes and chatting. I knew, suddenly, that I would never leave London again, a realisation that filled me with a sadness made pleasurable by the accompanying understanding that it was merely my ration of the melancholy we all shared during that long and long-ago war.

'It's hard, isn't it?' she said suddenly, as if reading my thoughts.

'What is?'

'Well. This.' And she gestured around feebly with her half-smoked cigarette. 'I fear that my heart has grown small and mean. It used to have more room for things. Those unnecessary things. Beauty. Love. A sense of wonder. It's all been squeezed out by desperation and the fear of imminent death, worrying about fresh food. All that's left are such thin pleasures.'

A stark analysis, but true. I looked around and made a sound of agreement. 'Are you afraid of death?'

She thought about this for a long time before answering. 'You hope it's quick, don't you? After all, as the Duchess

Season of Hope

of Malfi pointed out, we are sure to meet such excellent company on the other side. I would see my mother and father again. My friend Charlotte. She died early on. She couldn't take it. Can't say I blame her.'

'You really think there's another side?'

She sucked hard on her cigarette and, when she spoke again, grey smoke jetted from between her lips. 'I hope so. You know, I spent three hours last week helping a young girl find her cat. The poor creature was missing after an air raid and I foolishly offered to help.'

'That's not so foolish, is it?'

'I say foolishly because I saw the poor creature dead under some rubble almost as soon as I started looking, but I didn't have the heart to tell the girl. You have to give the kids some hope, don't you? Youth is the season of hope and all that. Even if it's just a black cat. It's something, at least, isn't it? I can't remember the cat's name now. Poor thing. Poor girl.'

Then Juliet and I heard the wail of air-raid sirens, almost detected the collective groan go up, followed by the scraping of chairs on lino floors as people stood from their kitchen tables, took a final sip of tea and headed down to the cellar or nearest shelter. I flicked my cigarette into the canal – half expecting the water to ignite, there was so much oil on top of it. But Juliet didn't move.

'I hate those fucking shelters,' she whispered.

I knew what she meant. There was something abject about crouching in the near dark with dozens of strangers: listening, identifying the types of bombs, trying not to pay attention to those eager to speak the names aloud, as if in so doing it afforded some sort of occult protection. *Whistler. C10, I think.* Pause, a collective flinch. *That's a . . . Scrambler.* I preferred not to know the names of the missiles seeking me; I hoped my own death would be a surprise. The ground shuddering, plaster trickling from the roof, a child coughing. *Close one, that.*

I stood up. 'Well. We probably shouldn't stay here,' I said to her eventually. My body was fizzing with adrenaline. It was not an entirely unpleasant sensation. Indeed, one of the stranger aspects of the bombings (and I'm not alone in this, for others have written of it, too) was the millenarian carnality it fostered.

The sirens wound down, then started up again. We had perhaps ten minutes before the bombs began to fall. Juliet stood and held out her hand. 'It's okay,' she said. 'I know a place.'

Juliet led me through the dimming streets to the Prince George. I thought the pub was long closed, on account of its boarded-up windows, but it had in fact become a venue for bacchanalian air-raid parties. My chagrin at being uninitiated into this little secret was more than compensated for by what I discovered inside. It was hot, sweaty and smoky. Condensation dripped from the ceiling. The atmosphere was charged with a desperate sort of pleasure and, best of all, the music was loud enough to drown out the noise of all but the closest bombs. People danced with abandon, a woman spilled liquor on my shirt, laughed and then kissed me hard on the mouth by way of apology.

Someone clapped me on the back and called my name. It was Donald, red hair sticking up all over the place, his face aglow. Juliet slipped from my grip and melted away into the throng. I lost sight of her. I tried to shake Donald but he would not be fobbed off and insisted I open my mouth.

'Why?' I yelled.

'Because acid,' he said and placed a tab of it on my tongue. 'Micky got hold of some of the old-school stuff . . .'

And it was done before I could think better of it, the hallucinogen washed into my body with a slug of beer. From there the night lurched away, spinning closer, then further, again closer, like a monumental carnival ride, all lights and frenzy, thrown gloriously off its axis. If the world were to end tonight, I thought, oh please, take me with you.

In the morning, or perhaps it was even the morning after that, I staggered from the Prince George into the street. My jaw ached and I felt like I'd smoked a thousand cigarettes, which, quite possibly, I had. So much had happened but I could recall almost none of it with precision. A conversation about clouds, I think, the intricacy of the broken bathroom tiles and a fellow dancing naked on a table.

Outside, the air was dusty and smelled of acrid smoke and smashed mortar. I heard a police siren drawing closer, voices yelling, shots. Not an uncommon sound in those days. Probably the police firing at looters; they had orders to shoot on sight. I listened some more. Nothing. Even the birds had abandoned the city. Things shimmered at the corners of my vision, glimpses of people, of leaves fluttering in the breeze.

A bewildered-looking girl walked past me calling for her cat. I watched her shrink into the distance. A girl looking for her cat. Just a girl looking for her cat. She would never find her pet, I thought, and this dead-end realisation filled me with sudden and acute despair. That's how it went: your friends would be killed, you'd hear of so-and-so vanishing, your house would be destroyed and you'd manage to contain all that terrible grief until a girl looking for her lost cat broke your fucking heart.

'What's the matter?'

It was Juliet, standing right beside me on the pavement. I'd hardly seen her during the night – or nights – of the party and yet her presence then seemed so inevitable and right.

I wiped tears from my cheeks. 'A girl looking for her cat.'

Juliet shrugged into her coat, fag hanging from her lower lip. With smudged eyeliner and her hair tousled just so, she looked wretched, beautiful, immensely desirable.

'Really?' she said in that husky voice I'd already begun to love. 'Where?'

I pointed along the street, towards Graham Road. 'Gone now.'

She stared down that way, then looked at me suspiciously. 'Did you take some of that acid, by any chance?'

I nodded.

'Ah. That explains it.'

'Explains what?'

She laughed. 'Do you have anywhere to go?'

Season of Hope

That summer I was living alone in the basement room of a bombed-out squat in Richmond Road, quite near London Fields. My water came through a garden hose hooked up to the place next door, and electricity was sporadic, to say the least. I could have found better accommodation but I lacked the wherewithal to do anything about my situation. In any case, it was hard to defy the superstition that a bomb wouldn't fall twice in exactly the same place, and I felt strangely protected there. Sometimes at night I watched the war on TV, eating Indian takeaway, drinking Special Brew, a blanket bunched over my shoulders.

I could have explained all this to Juliet but instead, mercifully, she threaded her arm through mine and I was spared the agony of articulating what she doubtless sensed anyway. She tugged me away from the corner. 'Come over to mine for a cup of tea, then.'

'Puckle,' I said, without thinking.

'What?'

'The girl's cat is called Puckle.'

She stopped. 'You're right. It *was* called Puckle. How did you know that?'

After leaving Juliet with Mr F that day in Brighton, I found myself pacing the boardwalk, trying not to think of what exactly he was doing to her. The intimate violence of the 'procedure' – as the intermediary had referred to it – made me feel queasy. I bought a chocolate ice-cream but was unable to take more than a few bites before tossing it into a bin.

The boardwalk was packed with couples and children. The ice-cream van played its sad, tinkling song. The air was mild and still, discoloured with a milky haze of smoke. I could smell burnt rubber on the sea breeze. All week there'd been rumours of a riot in the nearby Russian sector, dozens of people beaten and shot, but no one was talking about it in public. Life was hard that year, and not only for me.

Eventually, I stood at a rusted railing and stared out over the Channel. The water was grey. The wreck of the gunship *HMS Elizabeth* still lolled on a sandbank a couple of miles from shore. Gulls stalked the pebbly beach like twitchy, energetic derelicts, picking up and discarding cigarette butts and empty wrappers. Above the hubbub of the waves and the crowd milling on the sand, I heard a kid screaming in the distance, the rhythmic *tap tap tap* of a hammer. Life going on, despite everything.

An elderly man standing beside me gestured out over the beach with his yellowed fingers. 'Terrible, isn't it?' he said.

Unsure whether he was actually addressing me, I merely nodded in a way calculated to discourage him from including me in whatever prognostication he was preparing to make. My lack of enthusiasm didn't stop him, however.

'I remember when there used to be mermaids out here,' he said, waving his bony, nicotine-stained fingers towards the few blackened struts of the pier still poking up through the water like stitches through skin. 'Swimming in the shallows, lounging about beneath the old pier. Mermen, too. Whole families. At night you'd see them. So beautiful. So very beautiful. Their tails, their soft voices. Incredible.

Doesn't seem that long ago, really. Makes me cry to think of them gone, although I still expect to see them some day. I come down here most evenings, you know. Such a shame.'

I followed his gaze, unaccountably disappointed to see none of the creatures he had described. 'They'll be back,' I said.

He turned to face me. 'You really think so?'

I had no idea why I'd encouraged his preposterous fantasy, but his delight at the thought of the mermaids' return obliged me to persevere. 'Yes. I do think so. Why not?'

'Why not, indeed!'

We talked for a few minutes more before I bade the old man farewell and walked to a dingy pub, where I drank a pint of lager. By the time I returned to the hotel it was almost dark. There were very few people around and the narrow streets had gathered about themselves a menacing air.

In the room, Juliet was lying on top of the narrow single bed. Her face was very pale, but she smiled when I walked through the door and the sight filled me with almost inexpressible relief; part of me had expected the worst of the whole encounter. There were stories of rogues, after all – sinister tales of infection and malpractice.

'Never fear,' she scoffed with a thin smile, evidently seeing my relief. 'I do not plan on dying merely to provide a catalyst for your emotional narrative.'

'I can't fool you, can I?'

'Nope.'

She sat upright, with one hand on her brow, but I could sense her energy building, a little roiling storm about to break. She began to cry and I comforted her as best I could.

'There's nothing to say,' she sobbed, and I was relieved for, indeed, I could think of nothing to say.

I remember the faint smear of blood on the back of her hand, her fingers digging into my shoulder and, outside the window, streetlights rippling through the glass. That these should form part of my final memories of her fills me with tender grief, a bruise forever on my heart.

The next morning we took the train back to London. Although the city had not been bombed in some weeks, the streets were a mess. Debris, wrecked cars, the ruins of buildings and the smell of torn electrical wires. A woman on crutches made her way along the footpath, singing a hymn. A boy sold newspapers.

It was warm. A beautiful day, almost. Juliet and I made our way – by bus, then on foot – to our now familiar spot by the canal, where we sat on what we thought of as 'our' bench. The silence was immense.

After a while, we became aware of a curious, siren-like mewling. We peered around, searching for its source. There, among a pile of rags, was a black and white mother cat with her brood of four kittens clambering all over her.

We watched the little feline family for some time until, eventually, I opened my mouth to speak. I was preparing to say that we could take two of the kittens and perhaps give one to the little girl I'd seen searching for hers after the night of the air raid. The other we could keep for ourselves. We could take it home and look after it. All these thoughts in a split second, accompanied by fantasies of our kitten rolling about on the floor, tangling with a ball of wool, sleeping. Its soft fur, tiny ears.

But before I'd spoken a word, Juliet shook her head. 'No,' she whispered.

And she was right, of course, for how could we, really, expect to care for anything else when it was so hard even to look after ourselves? Foolish, sentimental thoughts.

We sat in silence for a while longer, watching the kittens.

And then – inevitably, it seemed – the moan of air raid sirens echoed through the late afternoon, but for the first time I felt no urge to escape, no desire for shelter. It seemed too difficult, too pointless.

Neither of us made a move to stand. After a few minutes, Juliet rummaged through the outer pockets of her overcoat, producing two coins, one of which she offered to me. 'Put this under your tongue,' she said. 'Just in case.'

I stared at the pound coin gleaming in my hand. I heard the drone of planes, blasts rolling nearby like approaching thunder, the tinkle of glass on a road. The mother cat had jumped up at the sound of the first explosions and was pacing about, her milk-heavy belly dragging on the ground, ears pinned back. Her kittens meowed tremulously and two of them had also leapt up and staggered drunkenly about. Another blast – this one much closer – and they shrank down, cried. Such tiny eyes, sodden fur, no idea of what was happening, just their terror. It was a heartbreaking sight, one of so many in those dreadful years.

'Do you remember that morning when you first took me back to your place?' I asked Juliet.

'After that wild party at the Prince George? Of course I remember.'

'And you made me tea?'

'Yes.'

I shook my head, fearful that if I tried to say anything else I would only weep. What could I say, anyway? How could I even begin to explain how the tea and the sight of its steam rising from the cracked cup in the morning sun restored me in ways I would never truly be able to fathom? Her skin so pale and warm, the distant sound of traffic.

The bombs were falling quickly now, arriving in crackling flurries, in the usual pattern. Falling all over Dalston and Islington, to judge by the sound of them, and almost certainly getting closer. Shortly it would be carnage: fire and blood.

Eventually, I was able to speak. 'Thanks. That's all I wanted to say. That's all.'

We each placed our coin beneath our tongues. A damp little clink of metal against teeth. Juliet took my hand and squeezed it. I sensed the action of her bones beneath the skin of her fingers; I sensed my own in response.

And by the canal we sat, so hopeful, so very hopeful, with money in our mouths the flavour of blood.

A Lovely and Terrible Thing

WHAT A BURDEN it is to have seen wondrous things, for afterwards the world feels empty of possibility. There used to be a peculiar human majesty in my line of work: the woman with hair so long she could wind it ten times around her waist; old Frankie Block, who could wrestle a horse to the ground; the boy with a fox tail. There was a good reason we referred to ourselves as The Weird Police. Now it's more likely to be a conga line of Elvis impersonators sponsored by McDonald's. Somewhere along the way the job lost its magic, but perhaps that's just me.

It was dusk when I pulled over to phone my wife. I would be gone for only two nights, but caring for our daughter Therese was gruelling, melancholy work, like tending to a fire perpetually on the verge of going out. More than once I had come home to discover Elaine sitting in the near dark, weeping with the endlessness of it all, and there was nothing

I could do but hold her until she felt better. It took hours, sometimes. Others, all night.

My phone didn't have reception out on the back roads. I trudged into a cold and muddy field with it held foolishly over my head, but it was no use; I would have to call from the motel in Kyneton.

When I returned to the car, the damn thing refused to start. I fished out a torch, popped the bonnet and peered at the engine, but the mass of wires and pipes might have been Sanskrit hieroglyphs for all the sense I could make of them. No cars passed. There was not a house in sight. I cursed my decision to take the scenic route. At least on the highway someone might have stopped and helped. On the highway my phone would have had reception.

I jiggled a few wires and checked the radiator, but it was no use. By now the horizon was darkening and the wind had turned sharp and bitter. Again I stared at the mute, incomprehensible engine and it occurred to me that a mechanic might have fared better with Therese than any of her medical specialists had over the years. I held my freezing hands over the engine, but the heat it gave off was minimal and diminished as I stood there.

I was beginning to resign myself to the prospect of spending the night in the car when a voice startled me. I swung around to see a large man approaching through the gloom. 'G'day,' he said again.

Embarrassed to have been discovered warming myself over a dead engine, I took my hands back and greeted him.

'Everything all right?' he asked.

I gestured to the engine. 'Car's broken down on me. I pulled over to make a phone call and now it won't start.'

The fellow was about my age, dressed in overalls, with a shock of grey hair that flapped about like a bird's broken wing. He stood nodding at the roadside verge and considered me for a moment. 'Want me to take a look?'

'Yes, that would be great. Thanks.' I held out my hand. 'I'm Daniel Shaw, by the way.'

The man grunted and shook my hand, reluctantly, it seemed. 'Dave. They call me Angola 'round here.'

'An*gola*. Like the place?'

He started. 'You've heard of it?'

'Of course.'

He paused. 'Well, I spent a few years there.'

He took my torch, positioned it on the rim of the bonnet where it would provide the best light, and set about poking around inside. After a few minutes he urged me to try the ignition again, which I did, but without any luck.

'Dunno, mate,' Angola said, wiping his hands on a rag produced from a back pocket. 'Reckon she's stuffed for now, though. Where you going?'

'Kyneton. How far is that?'

Again he looked at me as if puzzled to find me there at all. By now it was almost dark. The only light was from my torch which, at that moment, splashed its beam across the right half of his face. I imagined us from a distance – two men, strangers to each other, on a lonely road – and felt a jolt of fear.

'Too far to walk,' he said at last, above a roar of sudden

wind. He undid the bracket supporting the upraised bonnet, grabbed the torch and let the bonnet fall. 'But you can stay the night at my place, if you like.'

'I need to be there by two tomorrow afternoon. There's something I have to verify. I work for Ripley's Believe It or Not, and there's supposed to be a parrot that can count to a hundred and fifty. I have to check it's true. We might use it in the next annual.'

That piqued his interest. It usually did. Angola sauntered closer and looked me over. 'You work for Ripley's? Like the TV show? Ha. You musta seen some pretty weird things.'

I laughed. The world's most tattooed man, the girl with eighteen fingers, the ultra-marathon runners. He didn't know the half of it.

With his thumb he indicated the field beside the road, beyond which, presumably, he lived. 'My daughter has a pretty special trick, actually. Maybe you should come and see her? Put her in your big old book.'

He said this in a mildly lascivious manner I didn't care for but, as usual, that word pricked my heart, deflating it ever further. *Daughter*. I thought again of poor Elaine, poor Therese: my silent, waiting family. I hoped my wife had at least turned on the lights before pouring her first Scotch.

'You got kids?' Angola asked me, handing back the torch.

'Yes, I have a daughter, too, as a matter of fact.'

He grinned. 'Then you know what a lovely and terrible thing it is.'

It was an incongruous and curiously poetic description, particularly coming from his gap-toothed mouth. I nodded.

For a moment I could not speak. I looked off into the bleak distance, then at this man, and there was something in the sad shake of his head and the way his hair flapped about on his scalp that filled me with unreasonable warmth. A decent man out here in the country, with mud on his boots and the grease of a stranger's car on his hands.

For reasons best known only to the darker parts of myself, I felt immense shame about Therese, and rarely told anyone of my troubles; I had colleagues, for instance, who were completely unaware of her existence. But, for some reason, out on this road, I felt compelled to tell this man what had happened to her.

I coughed into my fist. 'But my daughter is – she was in an accident. Eight years ago. She cycled onto the road when she was eleven and got hit by a car. She lost the use of her legs and became brain damaged. We don't even know if she knows who we are – my wife and I, I mean. They say – the *experts*, that is – to hope for a miracle, that she might recover some of her movement and coordination. It has happened before, you know. Small breakthroughs, they say. Keep an eye out for small breakthroughs, whatever they might be.' I could have bored the poor fellow with talk of trauma and lobes and the ripple effect, but instead I tapped my head with my index finger. 'We don't really know what goes on in there.'

It was at this point that people usually said something consoling, along the lines of *I'm sure she'll come good one of these days*, but the man called Angola merely stared at me, listening, until I said all I had to say. And it was perhaps for this kindness that I enquired after the 'trick' of his daughter's. Normally I would not follow up on every stranger's claim — we all believed our children to be possessed of special talents, even those of us whose faith had been worn so thin — but I felt I owed him this courtesy.

Angola waved my polite query away. 'Oh,' he said. 'You'd never believe me.'

'I've heard some pretty wild stories, you know.'

He looked at me for a long time. It was unsettling. I saw now — by what light I couldn't say, for the sun had well and truly set — that his face was pitted with acne scars and his left earlobe was malformed. But there, by the road, he told me something so bizarre, and in such a strange manner — looking from side to side, shrugging, mumbling — that I had no choice but to believe him.

I carried the torch as we squelched across a field and ducked between the barbed wire of several fences. I asked him about Africa, but he was reluctant to disclose his reasons for being there and became sullen, saying merely that it was a terrible place and that he hadn't deserved to be there at all.

It was only when we saw the lights of his small house in the distance that I realised, and stopped. 'Your name,' I said, trying to keep the panic from my voice. 'It's not for the country, is it?'

My companion paused and wiped his meaty paw beneath his nose.

It was freezing. My shoes were sticky with mud. 'It's for the prison, isn't it? In America.' I recalled an entry from the 1972 Ripley's annual: an inmate who – although he had never left the state of Louisiana – built a precise scale model of central Paris from toothpicks, complete with street signs and roadside markets, tiny apples and pears.

'Course it is,' he growled, and continued walking.

I stared after him until I could barely make him out in the darkness. I pondered my options, which were few. A minute passed and I staggered after him.

Angola's house was large, but cluttered with thick-legged furniture, piles of toys and the detritus of domestic activity: mounds of knitting, fishing bags, a cricket set. Angola's wife Emma, elbow-deep in dishwater, seemed perplexed to see me in her house but shook my hand with her own sudsy one and offered me a beer. A teenage boy appeared and grunted at his father before skulking off. I peered around for the daughter about whom I had heard such amazing things, but there was no sign of her. Another son materialised, dutifully shook my hand and vanished. The television blared and I recognised the dopey voiceovers of *Australia's Funniest Home Videos*. The sons laughed themselves stupid at something. *I think I'll take a walk up here on the icy roof*... Angola and his wife bickered good-naturedly about an unpaid bill. *Boinggg*.

With their permission, I phoned Elaine from the dim, unheated study at the rear of the house. The windowsills were lined with children's sporting trophies. Football, cricket, tennis. *Best and fairest. Under 12 Champion*. The small desk was covered with bank statements, shopping catalogues, letters from a local school.

Elaine sounded harried – but not drunk, at least. Her words, already thickened by a French accent, were damp with unshed tears. Not for the first time I felt I might have been starring unwittingly in some mournful European film. She'd had a bad day of it: a tradesman had tracked mud into the house and then been unable to fix a pipe we had been waiting on for two weeks; Therese had to be changed three times.

'But she did a funny thing, Dan. You won't believe this but I went in this afternoon, she was in the sunroom – you know how she loves to stare at the birds at the feeder – and I swear she reached out to stroke my hair as I leaned over her.'

I paused to take this in. 'Are you sure?'

'Yes.'

'She stroked your *hair*?'

'Yes.'

This could be a breakthrough. I leaned forward, elbows on the desk. 'For how long?'

'Well. A few seconds.'

'It could be something, though, couldn't it?'

'Sure. Yeah.'

'It wasn't a –'

'Dan. I'm sure.'

Pinned to the wall above the desk where I sat was a child's drawing of a dog. Bulbous shapes conjoined by stick-like limbs, a scribble of blue cloud. I imagined Therese in her low bed staring at the ceiling where I had stuck luminous stars: her implacable face, her shining eyes. She might have contained entire oceans, shipwrecked galleons, dragons, concertos. I loved my daughter more when I was away from her; her actual presence only highlighted my inability to help her. My beery breath bounced back at me from the plastic receiver, and for the thousandth time since her accident I was flooded with sudden, acute disappointment at how I had so quickly reached the limits of my love.

I told Elaine I would be back the day after tomorrow at the latest, depending how long it took to get the car repaired.

'Dan?'

'Yes.'

'Do you promise?'

She often asked me that. 'Yes,' I said.

Returning to the lounge room, I passed a carpeted hallway I hadn't noticed earlier. Pop music drifted through a part-open door at the other end and a long matchstick of light fell on the swirling carpet. This must be the daughter's bedroom. I paused to listen, as if the music might offer a clue. Kylie Minogue. 'I should be so lucky'. Hysterical laughter from the lounge room, Angola asking his sons something. I shuffled down the hall towards the daughter's room. She was singing along to the music in a low voice. Despite myself, I sensed the thrill of discovering something truly incredible. What if her father had been telling the truth? I crept closer, almost holding my breath.

'You right, mate?'

I swivelled around to see Angola standing at the other end of the corridor. Although he was in silhouette, I could tell he was glaring at me. 'Yes, I was just –'

'That's Chloe's room.'

'Oh. I was, ah, looking for the bathroom.'

It was clear he didn't believe me. He wiped the back of his hand under his nose, then pointed the way I had come. 'That way. And dinner's ready.'

In any case, I didn't have long to wait before seeing the daughter. When I returned from the bathroom, the family was gathered at the dinner table and looked up expectantly at my entrance. The daughter, Chloe, was seated opposite me. She looked ordinary enough, but I couldn't help inspecting her whenever the opportunity arose.

Dinner was roast lamb with mint sauce and vegetables. Everyone talked at once. The boys bickered and thumped each other. Emma lit up a cigarette at the table as soon as she had eaten. Angola talked on his mobile phone for several minutes. The television raved away in the background. It was disconcerting to be at such a rowdy family dinner, but gradually, with the help of a few beers, I began to enjoy myself. *So*, I thought, *this is family life.*

Angola had cooled towards me, but I regaled the gathering with tales from my years as a verifier for Ripley's. Soon they were all laughing and wide-eyed, gasping in astonishment at South Pacific cargo cults, at the man who dived into buckets of water from great heights, the parachutist who shaved and smoked a cigarette in the time it took to float back to earth.

Angola picked something from his teeth. 'And do people make, you know, *money* out of these things?'

'Sure,' I said. 'Sometimes.'

At this, Angola's wife uttered an odd sound. I could restrain myself no longer and turned to the girl Chloe, who had been quiet the entire meal. 'So. Your father tells me that you have quite an unusual talent yourself? Would you like to show me what you can do?'

The family fell silent. Then Emma put her head in her hands. 'Jesus, Dave. I *knew it*. I bloody knew it . . .'

Angola started to protest, but his justifications were trumped by the only words I heard Chloe speak. 'No,' she piped, 'that's my sister Emily. She's in the shed.'

The shed was really a stable about one hundred metres from the house. A wind buffeted us as we made our way across the yard with a torch. I was anxious. Many years ago I met a woman who claimed to have a portion of Hitler's jawbone – complete with some piece of paperwork or other that verified it – but from the moment I stepped into her stinking, ramshackle entrance hall I knew she was just a lonely madwoman with a house full of junk. That I fell for it has long been a source of embarrassment for me, but in my business one needed to check all reasonable leads. Would this, perhaps, be the same? Or even worse?

Angola unbolted the massive door and swung it open. The stable was ill lit. Pausing on the threshold, I could smell wet hay and the sweat of animals. I knew the rest of the family were standing at the kitchen window, watching to see what I, a stranger, would make of their daughter. After Chloe had spoken up at the dinner table, there had been a heated discussion of money, of fame and reality TV that I did my best to dampen while still allowing them enough enthusiasm to show me their bizarre prize.

I stepped inside. Angola followed and closed the door behind me. Something stirred in a far corner; I heard a clank of chain. Angola brushed past me and went to another door on the other side of the stable. He paused with his hand on the wooden knob. 'You ready?'

I nodded. By this time my heart was hammering. The miraculous has a smell, and this godforsaken place was ripe with it. Angola opened the door and went in. Another rustle of chain, the swish of straw. Murmured words, kindly words. He beckoned me over. 'Don't be afraid,' he said, then to his daughter, 'This is Mr Shaw, love.'

I said hello and drifted into the room, which was spacious, decorated like any fourteen-year-old girl's room: posters of pop stars, family photographs, drawings of horses. The girl, Emily, was sitting on a low bed placed along one wall. She was slight, pretty, with long brown hair and large eyes. She looked momentarily startled, but quickly recovered, said good evening and smiled. It was clear we had interrupted her reading a book; it was placed facedown on the bed next to her. Then I saw the iron hoop around her ankle and the short chain attached at the other end to the bed frame. Emily noticed me staring at it and shrugged. Angola seemed anxious and asked her if she might show me her trick.

'It's not a trick, Pa,' she admonished.

Angola unlocked the iron hoop. 'Well. You know what I mean, love.'

A Lovely and Terrible Thing

Emily rolled her eyes.

Angola dropped the key to her bolt into his coat pocket and stepped back. He offered me an apologetic smile. 'Teenagers, eh?'

Emily swung around until both legs hung over the edge of her bed. Angola and I waited by the door. Horses moved around nervously in their stalls nearby.

'Are you sure, Pa?'

Angola nodded.

'But you said that –'

'Emily. This man might be able to help us.'

'Okay.'

And after a few minutes, it happened, as Angola had said it would. Almost imperceptibly, Emily began to levitate from the bed with no apparent exertion. The space between the hem of her dress and the rumpled bed expanded. Her face wore the expression of one absorbed in an interior activity like, say, listening to a favourite piece of music or contemplating a scene of sublime beauty. The entire thing happened in silence. When at last I could speak, I asked Angola how long she had been doing this.

'Oh, only two months or so. Not long.' It was clear that, behind his concern over what was happening to his daughter, he was very proud.

Meanwhile, Emily rose higher and higher. After several minutes, she put out a hand to prevent her head bumping against the high ceiling. Gently she shoved herself off, whereupon she drifted down and across the room before again floating to the ceiling. Finally, Angola took a length of rope, flung up it to his daughter and hauled her down to the floor, as one might a boat to a pier.

He secured Emily to her bed with the iron bolt. They exchanged tender words. He thanked her, kissed her on the forehead. We left the barn. Then he turned to me with an avaricious gleam in his eye, and I knew instantly what I had to do.

In the middle of the night, when I was certain the family was asleep, I eased the ring of keys from the hook by the kitchen door and crept from the house.

Emily didn't seem surprised to see me standing in her room. I sensed her looking at me as soon as I unlocked her door, but she said nothing, uttered not a sound. It was so quiet out there in the country I could hear her breathing in the gloom. I crouched by her bed and told her not to be afraid and she nodded as if she had known all along – known even before I did – what I intended to do. Some girls were like that. I unlocked the iron clasp from her bony ankle, gave her a moment to put a robe over her pyjamas, then lifted her from the bed and carried her outside.

My shoes crunched on the gravel driveway. I registered the familiar, pleasing sensation of a girl's warm and trusting breath on my neck, a cheek bumping against my shoulder. I had intended to carry her far beyond the edge of the property, but she was heavier than I anticipated – or I older and wearier – and I was compelled to put her down in the driveway seventy or so metres from the house. The girl gave a startled laugh, wobbled, then grabbed my sleeve as if momentarily unbalanced on a beam.

I held her by her wrist and we stood there for several seconds, staring at each other in silence.

'I'm scared,' she whispered.

'I know. But there is no need to be.'

The moon was high and full. By its light I saw the silvery outline of her jaw, tendrils of her hair waving in the breeze. Experimentally, I loosened my grip on her wrist and for a few seconds longer we stood there in the driveway, the girl and I, until she, too, let go of my sleeve.

I heard animals moving around us in the darkness, the soft and furry blink of their eyes. Emily smoothed her knotty hair and looked around. For a second I feared she would run or cry out for help but, instead, she looked at me and smiled. 'Goodbye,' she said.

Gradually, she rose into the air as she had done several hours earlier and the sight of it thrilled me anew. Her knobbly knees floated past my face and I realised I was weeping. She stifled a giggle with a hand across her mouth, then relaxed and held out her arms, and it seemed to me that she was not rising so much as the earth on which I stood was falling away beneath her feet. She waved. By the time lights came on in the house and I heard angry voices, the girl was already out of reach, floating above a nearby stand of gum trees.

Angola and his family ran up behind me with mouths full of oaths, but instead of escaping, as I should have done, I closed my eyes to better imagine the world from the girl's new height. I wondered if she saw trees in the distance, the yellow gravel of a driveway. Did she hear her father crying out and feel the stars close at hand, the vast and ancient universe into which she was being drawn? Far below, did she make out a man beating another man over and over with his fists, and hear a dog yapping at the commotion? People clawing at each other, throwing up their hands, shrieking?

Finally, when her family below fell silent and looked skyward, each of their faces glowed strangely and were so small they might have been coins at the bottom of a well as, free at last, she disappeared from sight.

Blood Brother

It's always summer in childhood. I remember when we went to see the Peanuts movie *Race for Your Life, Charlie Brown* for your birthday. Your dad dropped us off outside the cinema and we accidentally went into the wrong theatre and saw *The Deep* instead. It was 1977. We were nine years old. Lost treasure, Jacqueline Bisset in a wet t-shirt, harpoon guns.

We lived next door to each other until we were fifteen. We climbed to the tops of trees and all over the roofs of our houses – seeking a better view, I guess. Danger and escape from it. We could see a long way, perhaps not far enough. One hot afternoon we scored a gash in our palms with knives, smeared blood in each other's wounds and swore undying loyalty. An exchange. It was corny and it was true.

We collected dozens of cicadas in an old ice-cream container. We boiled and cut open a golf ball. In Manila we drank shakes made with condensed milk. More than once we stole your mother's cigarettes and smoked them in the back shed. We swam one summer weekend at Aireys Inlet and got into a rock-throwing fight with some older kids. We made slingshots from coathangers and rubber bands and shot at birds in trees. We ate plums straight from the tree, bitter, juicy. We made plans. Those countless Sunday mornings playing football when we were boys and, when we were older, shooting pool or playing pinball on weeknights at Johnny's Green Room. Smoking cigarettes, drinking coffee. 'Money for Nothing' always seemed to be on the jukebox – which makes it 1985 or so. The hours kicking a ball around in your backyard or watching videos of *The Deer Hunter*, *Star Wars*, *Taxi Driver*, *Apocalypse Now* and *The Graduate*. Endlessly, until we knew most of the dialogue. Are you trying to seduce me? You talkin' to me? Charlie don't surf.

I don't feel I have a right to miss you, not really, because we hadn't seen each other in years. I remember that day. The last time, that is. You, driving a taxi, sad and overweight; me, leaving my flat in Acland Street, St Kilda. This was probably in 1999. We were thirty-one. We made plans to catch up, but never did. You were at my wedding, but not really there at all; it was as if you had already left. But still. I do. Miss you, that is. And perhaps you of all people understand that you can't help feeling what you feel.

I'd heard of your troubles, of course, because our mothers are still friends and see each other regularly. Besides, it was our entire childhood, where everything really happens – the place where, as we age, we spend more time.

One afternoon I came home from school and you were waiting for me on the burning footpath, terrified. There was someone in your house, you said. A burglar or a murderer. We were probably twelve years old. Our older siblings were elsewhere, had most likely moved out of home by then. The parents were not around. It was different in those days; we had our lives and they had theirs.

From my place we grabbed a cricket bat and, having decided that entering through the back door was wisest, crept up the side of your house where the plum tree grew. The house was dark and cool, as always. The creak of old floors beneath the grey carpet. Did we call out or did we creep through room by room, opening cupboards and flinging things aside in our search for the intruder? We were excited, fearful of what we'd find.

The precise layout of the house is difficult for me to recall. I think your sister's bedroom was on the right, your own room on the same side but a little further along. There was a TV room, the dining room which was hardly ever used, the kitchen that overlooked our back garden. From that kitchen window we might have seen our dog, Winston, snuffling about in our back garden, maybe my odd sister sitting on the couch watching *Family Feud*, rocking back and forth.

I remember hearing of your death. A bad phone line, my mother weeping as she relayed the news, the cold air on the porch at my brother's place in the country where I took the call. Stars, the fog of my breath, the vast universe. The shiver in realising that a menace long eluded had at last slipped inside.

Often, in the middle of the day, I stop and think of what you chose to leave behind. The smell of dawn breaking over the ocean, the flavour of nectarine, a great joke, a catchy new song. I guess it wasn't enough.

Your note reached me several months later, after it was released by the police. They said you wrote it as the drugs took hold, but I don't know how they determined that. Thanks, but you never needed to apologise. I think that what you did was heroic in its way.

We found nothing, of course, that afternoon as we riffled through your house in search of the axe murderer, pulling our best kung fu moves and shouting *Ha!* as we kicked open doors and flung aside clothes. Afterwards we laughed and poured ourselves orange juice before going outside to kick the footy.

I was flattered you trusted me that day, that you thought me strong enough to help you. Because there *was* something hiding there, wasn't there? Somewhere we failed to look. I'm sorry we weren't able to flush it out and kill it. I was too young and you were too young. But, my friend, your blood runs in me still.

Crying Wolf

No one knew where the girl came from or even what her name was. My best guess was that Fat Ken the taxi driver had picked her and her boyfriend up in the middle of the night and somehow convinced them to come to Cecil Street to drop acid. This was a terrible idea; they were first-year university types who had only recently moved from the country. They had a fight almost immediately and the boyfriend vanished into the Fitzroy night in a huff. Meanwhile, the girl became convinced her scalp was bleeding, which of course it wasn't. At least I didn't think it was.

I had always been scared of acid (a little too nervy, too predisposed to apocalyptic fantasies of death and suicide and chaos) so I only took half a tab instead of the whole one the others took and, on account of this, the role of looking after everyone fell to me. I was to ensure no one did anything particularly idiotic or dangerous. I was in charge of playing records, making tea, stopping anyone from trying to cook or fly from the roof — that sort of thing. Which is how the girl became my responsibility.

Trouble was, I thought the whole thing was kind of funny and every time I tried to assure the girl that her head wasn't actually bleeding, I giggled — which only made her even more distressed. She kept rubbing her head and inspecting her hand for signs of blood. This was a bad little cycle to get into and soon she was sobbing uncontrollably and saying that she knew we were going to kidnap her and make her perform sordid sex acts. I felt sorry for her, I really did. Once after dropping acid I went to the Taxi Club at Taylor Square, which was full of gangsters and outlandishly dressed prostitutes. There was a large fish tank there and for hours I watched a massive, lipsticked groper that proved, only after some pretty intense inspection, to be a very obese transvestite leering at me from the other side of the tank. This was revelatory, like everything is when you're in that state (the world as metaphor or gateway, et cetera), and then there was a fight between some girls and their johns — broken bottles, blood, the whorl of police lights on the stairwell, the whole fucking catastrophe. I don't know how I got home but I couldn't leave the house for days and the sound of a fish tank's pump still gave me the heebie-jeebies. Which is a roundabout way of saying that acid is not for the faint-hearted, no.

Anyway. I had taken over the record player and was keeping everyone on their toes — swapping The The with Brian Eno, for example. A bit of New Order, that sort of thing.

Crying Wolf

And it was all going pretty well, notwithstanding the girl who thought her head was bleeding. A couple of people had wandered off to one of the bedrooms to stare at a quilt or something, but things were basically under control. Then the girl started saying she wanted to leave. Well, we couldn't let her go anywhere by herself, of course, but we didn't want to actually restrain her either – that would only freak her out even more. We fed her a jar of vitamin C tablets to try to bring her down, but that didn't seem to work, so I decided to go over to Dirty Dave's house and get some smack. Besides, it was pay day and it would be nice, so nice, to have something to take the edge off later, right?

I couldn't possibly leave the girl with the others, so somehow I persuaded her to come with me to Dirty Dave's, which was a few streets away. It was cold, and the night and its roofs and roads trembled at their edges like ivy in a breeze and I was reminded of something I saw in a movie or was it real life I couldn't quite recall, but it filled me with nervous joy. Dave answered the door in his undies and as soon as he saw me he knew what I wanted. It was late after all and, in any case, junkies are like countries – they have interests, not friends; a late-night visit could only mean one thing.

Dirty Dave was the kind of middle-aged loser who hung around in trendy pubs hoping that one of the young, beautiful women would be impressed enough by war stories from the old days to throw him a drunken fuck. He was bearded and shambling and a low-level sleaze, but he usually knew where to get hold of some good heroin. That. What?

He made the girl welcome and fussed about, making tea in his grubby, fluoro-lit kitchen while I explained as best I could, as best I knew, what had been happening. He even managed to rustle up some biscuits. The girl just sat there, touching the side of her head now and then and inspecting her fingertips for non-existent traces of her blood. She seemed slightly better for the short walk and I wondered whether the whole smack thing was really necessary but, of course, things had been set in motion and Dave had already made the call, leaving me alone with her – the girl, I mean.

The girl had in the meantime become creaturely, I guess you would say, and she paused to lick her narrow snout and run her inner wrist all across her face. She inspected her hands. Chipped red nail polish, very white fingers. She sort of growled in her throat, then stopped and shook her head. 'My mouth feels funny. Oh. Yes. That's right.' She paused, as if thinking deeply. 'My sister died, you know. Last year.' And she made a pistol of her forefinger and thumb, put it to her temple and puffed air softly through her lips. And then she began to weep, oh God, and there I was sitting next to her under the flickering fluoro and I never knew what to do in these situations. Basically, I was inept at being a decent human. Some people had a gift for consolation but I had no real idea and while I was wondering what on earth to do she thankfully pulled herself together. The fur on her cheeks glistened with damp tears and.

I ate a biscuit, reached out for one and placed it in my mouth, but it felt and tasted like dirt. The metal rim of the table glowed darkly, like a road at night seen from on high – there were cars with their lights, humming voices, signs, mansions. I thought, for long seconds, that I was god I was god your god yes rising above it all.

'Do you hear that?' the girl said, startled, glancing around so much like the little wolf she resembled.

I paused, was returned to myself. Nothing. 'What?'

'Where's my boyfriend?' she whined.

'He's gone.'

'Oh no. Really? When?'

Of course I had no clue. It might have been centuries ago, the dark ages, already tomorrow for all I knew. Then she leaned in towards me, all twitchy, and raised one admonitory finger like a thin and wickless candle. Shook her head and licked her lips once more. Her tongue a snake squirming in her mouth.

Next thing I know Dave is back with night air glittering all over him and he's got a spoon out and a fistful of fits and he's saying, laughing, *You guys haven't moved hardly an inch and who's going to do the girl I'll do it I don't mind.*

'What's it feel like?' the girl asked anxiously.

What could I tell her? That it was a bit of everything, all at once: sorrow, hunger, satisfaction, pleasure, need, beauty and terror. The most melancholy of all drugs. 'It's a bit like sleep,' was the best I could come up with.

'Oh, but much better than that,' Dave chided as he brandished a loaded syringe and rolled up his sleeve. 'It's more like death. In any case, it will fix any broken heart.'

And he was right – about death and broken hearts. The dig and prick, the ribbon of blood unfurling in the little chamber. There's much glory in that if you know where to look.

I was living behind an old shop on Brunswick Street. Its backyard was overgrown and full of broken things, bits of cars and furniture. Later, after dawn, I stood there gazing up at the lightening sky, at the hot-air balloons drifting high overhead, with rain on my cheeks like glass, like blood, like the warmest of all tears, and a horrible chill passed through all my bones.

I came back to myself on the carpet in Dave's hallway. Dust and rectangular cities, the smell of ancient braziers. I heard voices from the front of the house. Then I remembered the girl and sat up. The bedroom. Shit. The girl was alone with Dave. That wasn't good.

When I finally made my way up the listing hall, they were on the floor of the bedroom, munching on slices of apple and chatting like a pair of kids. On the carpet between them was a square game-board with odd writing and squiggly symbols on it. I lingered in the doorway, eavesdropping.

'But how will you know it's her?' Dave was asking the girl.

'I'll ask her about all the things I gave her. The ring. And all the little notes . . .'

Dave noticed me and nodded jerkily in greeting.

'What are you guys doing?' I asked.

The girl swivelled around. She grinned and her teeth gleamed in her wide mouth. She seemed transformed.

'Ah. There you are. Great. We need another person to do this properly. We're going to try to contact my sister.'

By this time my eyes had adjusted to the low light and I could see that the board on the floor was one of those ouija boards, for communicating with the dead, and Dave was murmuring, *Are you sure you want to know what you think you want to know?*

The girl waved his question away and signalled for me to join them. 'Come,' she whispered. 'Sit next to me. Don't be afraid.'

But I was, of course. Afraid, I mean. I always was.

Thankfully, nothing happened with the stupid ouija board. We sat in the gloom with our fingers balanced on an upturned glass and asked questions of the dead and waited, but there was no response. It was spooky and I was relieved when we decided to abandon it and go for a walk.

We wound up at Edinburgh Gardens, where it was dark and soft. Dave slumped on the crappy grass, exhausted from his short walk, then I guess he slunk off somewhere because I didn't see him again. It began to drizzle so I took shelter in the cabin of the decommissioned steam train that had been relocated there for kids to play on.

After a while I became aware of the girl sitting beside me, of the human warmth of her human thigh resting against my own. She seemed to have a coat I didn't recall her wearing before, but perhaps she had found it somewhere, or I had forgotten it? Blue suede, worn to a sheen at the shoulder.

A drift of perfume that seemed a reminder of something foreign. Blossoms, fields, sunny days.

I fumbled through my pockets for my cigarettes. I shook one out for myself and one for the girl and cupped my hands around a burning match until both were lit.

'I can feel the life in you,' she said as she sat back. 'The blood running through your veins. All contained in there. Do you ever think about that? About all the blood inside you? The veins and nerves and organs and cells.' She placed a palm to my chest. 'And that *heart*. In there behind that skin and all those bones. To think that, one day, perhaps quite suddenly, it will beat no more. Do you ever think about that?'

Most truths are awful, but this is perhaps the worst and greatest of them and I wished she hadn't spoken. After a moment she withdrew her hand. I missed it terribly. The world shimmered. I stared at the back of my hand, made a fist, unclenched, made a fist again. Veins and nerves and bones and cells, moving about unseen. We smoked in silence for a time, inhaling and exhaling like little machines. I sensed the presence of many people all around us. A woman, a dog, an old man in rags. Somewhere, a baby cried. I understood at once that they were the dead, going about their business. So many, of every age. I was strangely reassured by them, this glimpse of our shared fate. It made me feel less alone. So much I understood, there was so much to know. And then they were gone. I felt emboldened, gifted, filled with light. To be so alive and so very aware of death. Miraculous! Such pleasure, would I ever know one greater?

Ah, the acid. How much had I actually taken?

'What would you want to know, anyway?' I managed to ask after a while. 'If you could get a message to your sister? You know, with that ouija board?'

The girl ignored my question for a long time. She held out one hand. Rain pooled and glimmered like mercury in her palm. 'I don't want to know anything anymore,' she murmured at last. 'But I do miss this. The feel of rain, I mean. Sitting with handsome boys late at night. The possibilities. All of this is lost to me now.' She laughed sadly and rested her head on my shoulder. 'And I miss my sister, of course. Although she'll come to me eventually. Everyone does.'

A bird hooted nearby. The girl started and glanced towards it, and with her face turned to the streetlight, I saw that, yes, in fact, there *was* a greasy darkness at her temple. She clucked her tongue and wiped her head and, this time, when she inspected her hand, her fingers gleamed with blood.

'Jesus. You *are* bleeding,' I said idiotically.

'You cannot do what I have done without losing blood,' she said, perhaps quoting a poem or something – although, to be fair, everything had begun to pulse with mysterious meanings.

I noticed her as if for the first time; she was really quite beautiful. I thought, quite suddenly, that I'd like to sleep with her. Should I hold her hand or something? Put an arm around her? I could probably kiss her; there was nothing to stop me. But I'd always been pretty pathetic. Fuck. Did I say that out loud?

But then, reading my greedy thoughts, she asked, 'Do you have a girlfriend?'

Did I? Yes, more or less, although I was avoiding her at the moment. Only the day before, or it might have been the day before that, she had gone for an abortion at a clinic somewhere and, although I had given her money for the procedure, I hadn't gone with her – as I should have – because I was frightened of emotional things and most careless with people's hearts, my own included. But apparently it all went okay, which is to say the child would now not be born.

Anyway, I nodded. 'Yes. Sort of.'

She snorted. 'Men always say that.'

I sensed the girl looking at me strangely, perhaps unsure of what I was talking about – if I had been talking at all – but I was overcome, in any case bashful at the best of times, so I simply stared straight ahead at the trees dripping with water, at the lights of some distant, passing car.

'Do you love her?'

A shocking question. My friends didn't talk that way, never spoke of love or affection. The prevailing wisdom in the music we listened to or the books we read was that love was for the foolish, that it was dangerous and painful, perhaps even a disease that one might contract. But the girl waited and I was forced to mull it over. Did I love my girlfriend without knowing it? What did it feel like, anyway? Of course I felt things like pity, affection, lust, impatience or sorrow: a hand of cards that perhaps added up to something, depending on what the others at the table held. But love? That was like swallowing a lake.

The girl cleared her throat and seemed, mercifully, to lose interest in her question. 'When we were little, my sister and I used to dream different parts of the same dream,' she said after a while. 'I dreamed the head while she dreamed the body; I dreamed the river and she dreamed the bank; I the trees, she the leaves; I the rain, she the puddle; I the knife, she the wound. We assembled them in the morning before our parents woke up, like a puzzle. We used to tell each other everything. Her name was Sarah but my father called us Phobos and Deimos. The twin moons of Mars, apparently. Panic and dread, although we were never sure who was who. I was panic, most likely. But now I feel that I've abandoned her.'

'Should we go to the hospital or something? You know, about your head?'

'No. It's always like this now.' She gestured tiredly towards the horizon, where night was handing itself over to the pale summer dawn. 'But I think you should go back, before it's too late. Do you know the way?'

'Of course.'

'Because coming here is the easy bit, you know. Getting back is hard.'

She rummaged around in her coat pocket and held out a handful of items: scraps of paper, mostly, but also a few coins and a ring. 'Here. Take this ring. It might help you.'

I did as she asked. It was a woman's gold ring set with a small, reddish stone. It didn't look terribly valuable but I might still be able to pawn it at Sullivan's on Smith Street.

She considered the other items in her palm before returning them to her pocket. 'What's her name?'

'Whose name?'

'Your girlfriend.'

'Oh. Her name is Jane.'

'Ah. You know, I see *everything* now. Everyone's life and their death. All that has happened, laid out on all sides like a massive garden. This is why we're right to be fearful of death. The world collapses, grows infinitely larger. It's all too much to bear.'

She sighed. Silence. Then, answering a question I hadn't even asked, she said, 'Later, you will remember all this and you'll stare at the sky overhead and rain will fall on your cheeks like glass, like blood, like the warmest of all tears. You'll live for a long time yet, but you'll never really be a good man. These very nights and days, the ones you're living right now, will hang heavily around your neck.'

And, with that, she drew her coat around her, jumped down from the train cabin and loped away on all fours between the trees. It grew very quiet and I felt inexplicably marooned. The world and all it contained – its people, the cars, the houses and oceans and air – had drained away.

Sometime later, I found myself back at the house in Cecil Street, where the girl was sitting by herself on a milk crate in the tiny backyard. But wait – hadn't she gone home? Whatever. We chatted, but she didn't know where Dirty Dave or anyone else was. Why would she? I made coffee and handed her a cup. The old Greek neighbour muttered to herself over the fence. I hoped we hadn't made too much noise last night. My mouth felt truly horrible, wet and sticky, an open sore.

'How's your head?'

The girl touched her long hair. 'I think it's stopped, thank God.'

She looked quite good, actually; drugs suited some people, others not so much. I, on the other hand, felt woozy, as if I alone had carried the darkness all through the night.

'Are you okay?' she asked. 'You don't look so good.'

I had a dose of hepatitis and looked quite yellow sometimes, but I didn't tell the girl anything about it; it was a very grubby-sounding disease and it put people off. Taking drugs, of course, only made it worse; sometimes I pretty much glowed. And so I just shrugged and rested in the sun beside the fence.

'I'm sorry about your sister,' I said eventually.

'Pardon?'

'Your sister. Sarah?'

She shook her head. 'No, I'm Sarah. My sister is Josephine. Was Josephine, I mean. People used to get us mixed up all the time when we were kids. Our father called us Phobos and Deimos. They're the twin moons of Mars . . .'

'You told me.'

'But she's dead now.'

'You told me that, too.'

'Ah. I did?'

'Remember? At the park. And that you were probably panic.'

'No, no. I was *dread*.' She sipped her coffee and scowled. 'I knew she was going to do it one day. We all did. She went through terrible periods when she would talk about it all the time. I put notes in the pockets of her coats, hoping she would find them and not go through with it. *I love you. Hang in there*, that kind of stuff. Corny things, I guess. Poems. *This will pass*. Didn't work, though. Obviously. Our mother died of cancer when we were ten years old and she was the most beautiful woman we ever knew. Very stylish, kind, loving. We kept a ring of hers and shared it between us. We felt the ring had been invested with her love. With her spirit. Our dad told us that. Whoever was feeling bad could wear it, then put it back into the box when they felt better and then the other sister could wear it. We never spoke about it. We didn't need to. It just evolved that way. It was our thing. It's a twin thing. I put it in her coat pocket that morning. I thought it might help. That it would keep her here with me. That she would find it and be surprised and she would wear it and it would all be okay. You want to feel like you've done something, don't you?' She paused for a moment. 'Love is someone you keep returning to, isn't it? Someone that destroys and rebuilds your heart over and over again.'

This made me think, painfully, suddenly, of Jane. I should find her and see if she was all right. She would be really pissed off that I'd spent the night getting stoned without her. I'd have to apologise for it, not to mention for everything else I'd done or not done in the past few days or months. There would be tears and slaps, like always.

Then I had a thought. I could give her the ring! Surely it would make her feel better, if only for a little while. It wasn't much, but it was something, wasn't it? The girl was right – you do want to feel like you've done something. The ring was snug in my fist where I sensed its reassuring warmth. Some things did have power, or could be invested with power – like talismans, like magic. I would tell her I'd bought it for her. A gift. As a kind of apology. It was some consolation, wasn't it?

By this time the night was utterly vanquished; the sky was clear and blue, so full of promise. Yes. It was time. The strange girl was absolutely right: love is someone you keep returning to. That's exactly what it was. And now I would return to my girlfriend. To Jane. I gulped the rest of my coffee and stood up to go. I was suddenly filled with vigour and wild purpose. Yes. There was work to do.

'You got more of that stuff?' the girl asked.

'What?'

'That drug. Was it really heroin? It was so nice. And I've got money.' Clumsily, she produced a purse bursting with cash.

I dropped the ring back in my pocket. 'Sure,' I said.

Jane could wait another day.

The Deep End

MEREDITH HAS BEEN at the house for only two days, recuperating (from the affair, the procedure, et cetera), when she sees the boys emerge from the overgrown garden at the back of the property like a pair of little savages. It's almost dark, but her years as a high-school teacher have given her, if nothing else, an eye for the ages and personalities of boys and girls. These two are probably about fourteen or fifteen years old, both barefoot and wearing shorts. One of them is wearing a blue Rip Curl t-shirt but his friend is shirtless, quite lovely, with movements so quick and decisive. She watches them. They are so unlike girls, she thinks, with their brittle self-consciousness, their discussions and consultations, interminable instructions on the correct way of doing things. No. Her eye is drawn over and again to the shirtless one, whose hair is licorice-black with sweat, whose shoulderblades jut like fins from his back. And she knows. Knows even before she knows.

Her friends, the Coopers – probably the only friends she has left in the world – assured her their house in the tiny coastal village was relatively isolated and she would not be disturbed but, despite the potential for further scandal (wouldn't the press have an absolute field day to see her now?), she is delighted at the unexpected appearance of the boys. After all, solitude has never been her forte. She steps back from the upstairs window before they notice her, and peeks from behind the orange curtain. Cowering, she thinks with a sudden rush of bitterness. Cowering in the shadows like a common criminal.

From her vantage point she watches the boys approach the swimming pool. The pool is empty of water, except for a brackish puddle at the deep end that has, by some miracle, resisted evaporation in the summer heat. A green plastic tarpaulin has blown in and formed a makeshift tent over this miniature swamp. At night she has heard the tarpaulin crackle in the breeze, like a creature shifting its great weight. Sitting in one of the plastic chairs beside the pool smoking cigarettes, as she has done each evening since her arrival, one cannot avoid the smell of hot plastic and rotting leaves, a sharp and unpleasant mingling of the artificial and organic. There are fine bones and hanks of fur on the pool's pale-blue floor – the remains of mice or possums that have tumbled in, perhaps lured by the puddle of water, and been unable to escape. Meredith imagines them fumbling in vain for purchase on the curved sides (high-pitched squeaks, scrabble of little claws) before collapsing into exhaustion. This image of their last moments is strangely satisfying.

Still, it would be a grim end – dying in a rectangular, blue desert, edges of the pool melding seamlessly into the sky.

Meredith smiles as the boys go about their blunt, boyish business. It's so hard not to love them. The shirtless one scratches at his stomach. He kicks a shard of broken tile, swaggers around like a pirate with his little gleamy grin. They lurk about the edges of the pool for a while longer – squatting on their haunches, bickering in that sullen way, spitting, chucking rocks at things – before wandering back into the forest beyond, slashing at leaves with sticks as they go.

The cicadas' urgent chorus starts up, reaches its pulsing crescendo and falters. Then silence, abrupt and complete. She stands at the window for several minutes longer, wondering if she has imagined the boys, conjured them somehow from the forest. Although almost night, it is still terribly hot. My God, she thinks, I need a cold shower.

Jason makes sure Oscar has gone into his place for dinner before he dashes into his own house a few doors along, grabs a shirt and doubles back along the old ranger's track. His dad is having drinks with Mr McKenzie at the surf club and won't be back for a while. His older brother Matt is probably still at the beach. There is half an hour or so before he has to be home.

He scuttles along in a half-crouch, leaping over fallen trees, occasionally stubbing his toes on rocks, hair sticky across his eyes. It's dark by the time he finds his way back to the Cooper place. Once there, he hovers uncertainly among the vines at the edge of their property for several minutes, watching, his heart humming in his chest. Sweat prickles on his skin.

Although not acquainted with the Coopers, he's roamed through their house twice over the winter just passed. As a lifelong resident of the seaside village, he feels proprietorial over the houses owned by snooty city folk who only stay for a few weeks over summer or the occasional weekend. The Coopers' spare key was hidden in a fake foam brick in the wooden shed at the side of their place. Not the greatest hiding spot, but it's definitely not the worst, either; the McGills hide their spare key behind a tile right beside their back door. Jason's not entirely sure what he's hoping to find on these little incursions, but the frisson of handling Mrs Cooper's thin summer dresses hanging in her wardrobe or eating potato chips from the kitchen cupboard is reward enough. Once he stole a pair of sunglasses but was too afraid to wear them outside, and eventually threw them away. Another time, at the ramshackle Farnsworth place on Sunrise Avenue, he was thrilled and repulsed to find a jar of Vaseline in a bedroom drawer, and sat on the edge of the bed staring at the creamy goop (raising it to his nose, incredulous at its apparent lack of discernible scent) for what felt like hours.

The Coopers haven't come down this summer – something about Mrs Cooper's mother being ill, according to Bert Loomis at the petrol station. Who, then, is the woman he has seen peering from the top-floor window before sliding away behind the curtain?

A light goes on at the side of the house, where the bathroom is. He waits, but there is nothing more. He can hear the subterranean boom of waves as their rounded shoulders pound the shoreline, and smells a barbecue underway nearby. The smell of sausages cooking makes his mouth water and he wonders if he shouldn't go home. But after prevaricating for a minute or two he moves towards the house, skirting along the boundary, softly humming the theme from *Raiders of the Lost Ark* as he goes.

Years ago, Meredith had a boyfriend who told her she was like a cartoon from the *New Yorker* – those ones that feature raccoons in a psychologist's office reading the newspaper, or guests at an elegant party drinking cocktails and referring, in a witty but disparaging manner, to their publisher. This description was one she took immense pleasure in until one night, with a horrible start, she realised that the boyfriend in question (Bradley Jones, with his monobrow and callused hands, a fucking *builder*, who'd never even heard of the *New Yorker* until he met her) had intended it as an insult.

Bradley Jones – what a mistake he was. No way to get those eight months back, was there? The memory of him activates a little jolt of resentment deep within her, like a fire long thought extinguished flickering unexpectedly back to life. And this triggers a weird flurry of unconnected memories – like the time she fell asleep on her friend Farrah's couch after drinking too many bourbons; the view from a lodge she stayed at years ago in Tasmania with another boyfriend – what was his name? – Will Canston; the bizarre flavour of salted licorice she tried during her year in France.

Meredith is wondering about the randomness of memory as she showers, soaping her arms, when she looks up and sees a spooky little face in the lower corner of the bathroom window. She gasps and moves to cover herself before recognising it as the shirtless boy from earlier that evening. The dropped bar of soap lodges in the plughole, and water, tepid and waxy, dams up over her toes. Her alarm subsides into a more pleasurable sensation, one made more piquant by the nimbus of fright still at its edges. She pushes wet hair from her face and peers through the steam at the boy, smiles. He's certainly brave, this one. My God. Some of them, she thinks, you have to reel in ever so carefully, while others you can't keep away. But by the time this thought has articulated itself, the face has vanished, like a smoke ring disintegrating at the precise moment of its formation.

The garage is sweltering and stinks of engine oil and his dad's cigarettes. Jason switches on the yellow overhead light and picks his way through the old surfboards and boat parts. He pauses to turn over in his mind the image from last night, of the woman in the shower. Not that he could see much through the steamed-up window. Just the shape of her pink body, but that was enough. A row of shampoo bottles. And — it seems impossible — did she *smile* at him?

His trap is under the bench, which itself is scattered with tools and fishing equipment. It's simple, but effective. An ancient wooden box, part of an old meat safe, and a wire mechanism with a hunk of strawberry attached to a hook that connects to a door fashioned from part of an old bookcase. If anything tugs on the strawberry, the door slams shut.

He sees immediately the door is closed and, as always, his heart jumps a little. He kneels down and peers through the wire side. There, in the corner, hunches a black rat. The creature stares at him, nose twitching, eyes darting from side to side. Its little pink fingers pluck at the floor of the box, like an old lady worrying at her knitting.

'Hi, little fella,' he whispers. 'Have I got a surprise for you.'

Jason fetches a canvas sack, positions the opening around the door of the trap, slides the door open slightly and angles the box. No movement. He tilts the box further and jiggles it. Sure enough, he is rewarded with a scrabble of paws against wood as the rat slides into the sack. Holding it carefully, he ties off the top with cord. The rat struggles momentarily, then falls still.

Meredith is sitting in one of the plastic pool chairs when she becomes aware of the boy loitering at the edge of the property. Although it is almost dark, she hasn't yet switched on the outside light and the evening air has taken on an aquatic quality, as if the ocean has stolen ashore. She has spent the day lounging around, reading, listening to the radio, and the skin on her face is tight with light and sun. She is wearing one of Madeleine Cooper's sundresses and feels dishevelled, dangerous – but gloriously, fashionably so – like a woman from a Fellini movie. She pretends not to notice the boy for several minutes, then turns towards him and says, 'Hi,' as if his appearance were of no great note.

The boy doesn't say anything (teenage boys rarely do; it's part of their appeal) but nor does he run off. A good sign. She slaps at a mosquito on her calf and lights a cigarette.

She waits a while before addressing him again. 'Hey. Can I ask you something?'

The boy hesitates before coming nearer. He shuffles to the edge of the paved poolside area but seems reluctant to come any closer, as if the terracotta tiles marked a border. Like yesterday, he is barefoot.

'I was thinking,' she says, indicating the almost empty pool with a jab of her lit cigarette, 'of cleaning this pool out. I thought I might fill it up with water, you know. Would you like to help me? It would be nice to swim in this heat, don't you think? Together we could probably clean it out in a day or so. Scrub the sides down and fill her up again?'

The boy scowls, shakes his head. 'I wouldn't get into this pool.'

'You don't like to swim?' she asks after a confused silence.

'No. Yes. It's not that.'

'Then why?'

The kid looks undecided, then shakes his head again.

Meredith taps the ash from her cigarette, decides to change tack. 'Do you live around here?'

'Fairview Street.'

This address doesn't mean a thing to her, but she nods anyway. She's never been to Fraser Bay before and, having arrived at night in her hire car, she's still uncertain of the geography of the place. 'What's your name?' she asks.

'Jason.'

'Well, hi, Jason. I'm Meredith.'

The boy nods and mutters a greeting.

'Can I ask you a big favour, Jason?'

'Sure.'

'Can you not tell anyone you saw me here?' she says at last.

This grabs his attention. He scrutinises her. 'You hiding out?'

'Not exactly.'

'You famous?'

She laughs without humour, and hesitates before answering. 'Something like that. No. It's just that – how can I put this? – people don't always understand the friendship between a woman and a boy, if you know what I mean?'

'Are we friends?'

'We could be.'

'Tell you what,' he says after a thoughtful silence, 'I won't tell anyone I saw *you* here if you don't tell anyone you saw *me* here.'

Perfect. She holds out her right hand. 'Let's shake on it.'

The boy (so shy, so determined to disguise his shyness) steps towards her and they shake hands. She notices he walks with a slight limp.

'What's the matter?' she asks.

'Splinter.'

'Let me have a look.'

He turns to her and in the half-light his face has a lunar glint. She can smell him, sweaty and ripe.

'It's too dark to see now,' he says.

She takes a lengthy drag on her cigarette. 'Dusk is my absolute favourite time of the day. The light here reminds me of France.'

The boy looks impressed. 'Have you been there? To France?'

'I did an exchange year during high school. And I teach French now. Or I did.'

'But not anymore?'

She makes a dismissive gesture.

'How old are you, then?'

'Didn't your mother tell you it was rude to ask a lady her age?'

He grins and hoists his right foot up until it rests on his opposite thigh. He picks at the grubby sole with one hand gripping the back of a chair for balance, folded at the waist like a pale question mark in the gloom.

But she is reluctant to abandon this line of questioning. 'How old do you think I am?'

He lets go of his foot and considers her. 'Twenty-five or so?'

'Wow. Twenty-five. Absolutely right. I had a feeling you knew a little something about women.' And she is gratified to see how pleased he is at this remark. It's amazing how far a little flattery can take you. The balmy evening air, a lovely boy and the glass of wine combine to make her more reckless than usual. 'And how old are you?'

'How old do you reckon I am?'

'Ah. Touché.' She studies him. There is a scar on his left knee. Quite a long scar, from a shard of glass, perhaps, or a surfing accident. 'I think you are . . . at least sixteen.'

He shrugs, lets go of his foot. Doesn't correct her if she is wrong.

'Did you get the splinter out?'

'Nah. Can't see properly in this light.'

'Come on, then. Let's go inside and I'll look at it. There's probably some tweezers somewhere.'

'No, it's all right. Besides, my feet are pretty dirty.'

By now she is standing. She holds out her hand to him. 'That's okay. We're friends, remember? You can take a shower first. Then I'll take a look at you.'

He takes a step back. 'No. I'd better get home.'

'Are you sure?'

'Yep.'

'Maybe tomorrow, then?'

'I think the splinter will be gone by then.'

'Oh. Of course. Well.'

The boy drifts away shyly and has almost been absorbed into the leafy darkness when he turns towards her, his face hovering in midair like a little spectral moon. 'Whatever you do, don't go into that pool, okay?'

Puzzled and a little spooked by this warning, Meredith drops her cigarette butt into her empty wine glass and walks over to the edge of the pool, where she is greeted by a hot exhalation of mildewy plastic. Several bats glide overhead. By the time she looks back, the boy has gone. She waits a few minutes, to see if he will reappear, then goes inside and locks the door behind her.

*

After a late breakfast Jason leaves his house, crosses the dirt road and plunges through the hedge of ti-trees. He cuts across the abandoned lot where the Wheeler place used to be and lingers near the back fence of the house Oscar's family have rented for the summer. It's much nicer than Jason's place; they've got air-conditioning and a wooden deck out the back with a massive gas barbecue. You can smell the sea from here, those leathery skeletons of kelp sprawled on the sand.

Oscar is in the backyard, mucking around with a remote-control car. Jason watches him for a while. He gnaws on a thumbnail, spits out the shard of skin that he tears off. Remote-control cars always sound so great but they never work that well. This one of Oscar's is no exception, refusing to go any further when it encounters the slightest obstacle. Which, in an unkempt back garden like this one, is about every two seconds.

Finally Jason steps into the garden, reveals himself. 'You should take it down to the beach,' he says, 'where it's on flatter ground.'

Oscar looks up, surprised, squinting against the bright sun. 'Oh, hi.' He turns his attention back to the remote-control unit in his hand. He works the little rubber lever with his thumb. There is a whirring sound and the plastic buggy lurches forward, crashes into a brick and flips over.

On the deck Jason notices what appears to be a brand-new tackle box and fishing rod. The reel on the rod looks like the green Daiwa one he's had his eye on for ages at the general store. 'That your rod?' he asks.

'Dad got it for me yesterday.'

Jason sidles over to the deck and picks up the rod, hefts it in his hand. He fingers the metal bracket, lifts it and nods approvingly at the satisfying tension against his thumb. Lovely little thing, he thinks, and is startled that the phrase that comes most readily to mind is one his father would use. In the corner of his eye, Jason senses movement through the glass doors that open onto the rear deck. It's Oscar's mother — tall, brown, wet-haired — gliding past with a glossy magazine in her hand. She pauses, stares out and says something over her shoulder. And then, like an exotic sea creature glimpsed at the water's surface, she returns to the depths of the house shuttered against the morning sun.

'We could go fishing tonight,' Jason says. 'I'll take you to this spot up along the river. Catch tons of whiting.'

'Oh, yeah, that'd be excellent.' Oscar chucks the remote-control unit onto a chair. 'Is that where you were going the other night?'

'What?'

'After we'd been to that house with the empty pool. You were running along that little track.' Oscar points to the upper storey of his house. 'I can see your place from my bedroom window.'

Jason stares up at the window Oscar indicated, calculates the sightlines of the view. He should be more careful.

'It looked like you were in a hurry,' Oscar says.

Jason hesitates. 'Yeah, I was going fishing.'

'So what's the best time to go? Tonight, I mean.'

'Um. Six or so is probably the best. Tide'll be turning then.'

He assumes a fencer's stance and slashes the rod through the air. 'Can I use this tonight? For a while, at least?'

Oscar hesitates. 'Don't you have one?'

'Yeah, but. I thought. Like in exchange for me taking you to a special place and everything? And I'll get the bait.' Jason's voice falters and he is flooded with sudden contempt. This kid wouldn't know the first thing about fishing, probably can't even cast or anything – even with his fancy new rod and reel.

'Sure,' Oscar says, hopping onto the deck. 'I'll ask my dad. Let's get a drink.'

They step through the sliding doors into the kitchen but Oscar vanishes immediately in search of his parents and leaves Jason standing by the laminated bench like a servant. He has never broken into this house – he hasn't been able to find the spare key, if there is one – but relishes the shiver of transgression that seeps through him. His skin tingles, his bladder constricts. It feels as though his senses are more acute than usual. The kitchen is cool and light. The radio talks quietly to itself. There's a bowl of fresh fruit on the wooden table. A magazine, perhaps the very magazine Oscar's mother was carrying a few minutes ago, lies abandoned on a chair. Eventually, Jason ventures up the dim hallway towards the burble of conversation.

A woman's voice. The mother. 'Oh, I don't know, honey. We don't really know this boy . . .'

Oscar's father speaks up. His voice is deep and English-sounding. 'What's his name again?'

'Jason,' says Oscar.

'Oh, he's all right, isn't he, Margaret?'

'He seems,' Oscar's mother says, her voice dropping almost to a whisper, 'he seems like a little ratbag to me, to be honest. Looks absolutely filthy. Sort of skulks around. Fellow down the road told me the family is always making trouble . . .'

There is an intimation of movement from the bedroom. A drawer is closed. Jason bolts back to the kitchen, where he stands again by the bench, hoping to appear as if he has not budged an inch in the intervening minutes. But Oscar doesn't materialise. No one does.

Unnerved, Jason gazes through the glass doors, at the new fishing rod gleaming in the late-morning sun, at a pair of swimmers and a towel hanging on the back of a deckchair. Inside, on the kitchen bench, is a thick, gold bracelet that Oscar's mother probably removed to do the dishes or something. Jason stares at it. He listens out for voices, for footsteps. Nothing. Then, without further thought, he scoops up the bracelet and drops it into his pocket.

The question comes out of nowhere and takes Meredith totally by surprise. They are in the kitchen, standing by the bench. It's early evening, but still hot. She's on her third glass of white wine and Jason is sipping from a can of warm Coke he dug out of the cupboard.

'Why don't you teach French anymore?'

A moth dings against the light globe overhead. She pauses with the glass of wine halfway to her mouth, stunned. Had there perhaps been something in the newspaper? Her face is reflected back at her in the large window and she watches herself sip her wine, cautious now, before placing the glass on the table. 'How do you know that?'

'You told me.'

'I did?'

'Yeah. The other night.'

Her mind whirrs. 'Really?'

He nods and swigs from his can. Coke trickles down his chin and drips onto his t-shirt. 'You said you *used* to teach French. But not anymore.'

Meredith considers the bracelet he gave her earlier. Gold jewellery is not really her style, but it was sweet of the kid to think of her. The evening, quite suddenly, feels electric with possibilities. 'I'm not really sure I should tell you.'

'Why?' Jason looks at her, holds her gaze for several seconds. He's growing bolder each time he comes around. Nibbling away, like a fish on the line. Getting hungrier every day.

'It's nothing really, just . . .'

'What?'

She's surprised to feel a warm blush creep up her neck. A nervous laugh bursts from her and she waves a hand, as if batting away a fly. 'Oh, I kissed a boy, that's all. He was a student in one of my classes. And the principal didn't take too kindly to it. He's an . . . old-fashioned guy, I guess you'd say.'

She watches him swig his Coke as he incorporates this new information into whatever impression he's already formed of her.

The Deep End

'How old was this boy?' he asks after a pause.

'About your age.'

'What did he think about it?'

She laughs again, feeling tipsy and confident. 'Oh, I think *he* liked it.'

'Then that doesn't sound too serious,' Jason says at last.

'I wouldn't have thought so.'

'I mean. I wouldn't really mind if you kissed me.'

'Oh. Is that right?'

'Yep.'

She pours another wine, barely disguising the tremble in her hand. Sauvignon blanc splashes on the table. 'Oh. Maybe a little one, then.' Pauses. 'Why don't you come over here.'

Jason clears his throat and shuffles over until he stands in front of her. He is breathing heavily. A whiff of salt water. She trails her fingers across his smooth cheek, then tilts his face up towards her own and kisses him on the mouth. She feels the hard pulse in his lips. He nuzzles at her, seeking more, but she pushes him away, gently, a palm pressed to his chest.

'Easy does it,' she says. 'We have plenty of time. Now. I think you should tell me a secret, since I've told you one of mine. Something you've never told anyone. Even your friend.'

He blushes and backs away, clearly staggered at the turn of events. 'What friend?'

'The one I saw you with here. A few nights ago.'

'He's not my friend. His parents have rented a holiday place in our street, that's all.'

'Oh, all right. Anyway. Tell me something you've never told anyone.'

'Okay,' he says at last, holding out his hand. 'Come outside. I'll show you something.'

'Ooh, sounds exciting.' She allows herself to be led into the garden, where dusk is falling.

He dashes off, rummages around in the bushes at the far end of the property and returns a moment later with a small canvas sack.

'What's that?'

'You'll see,' he says, walking around the edge of the pool towards the deep end and dropping to one knee to loosen the knot securing the sack. He glances up to make sure she is watching before releasing something down the sloping side and into the mostly empty pool.

The object, about the size of a fist but dark brown or black, lands where the pool bottom dips down to the deep end, beside the bunched-up tarpaulin and the disgusting swampy puddle. The boy's contrived air of mystery seems to outweigh the drama of his little secret and Meredith is preparing to return inside and pour another glass of wine when the object moves, revealing itself to be, in fact, quite a large rat.

'Ugh,' she murmurs.

Jason puts a finger to his lips and gestures back to the pool. The rat is still, only giving itself away by the twitching of its pinkish snout. After a minute or so, it darts forward a short distance before stopping. Naturally enough, the poor creature has no idea how it ended up in an empty pool.

A few minutes later, Meredith senses another, more elegant movement near the tarpaulin. She squints through the half-light. It's hard to distinguish specific objects among the detritus collected at the lowest point of the pool. There are branches, a few rocks, some rotting leaves. And the tarpaulin, of course.

'Here he is,' Jason murmurs.

When the snake appears she is so mesmerised she is unable to speak. Just an unwitting gasp, a hand to her mouth. She watches as the snake, sliver of black tongue flickering in and out of its grim little mouth, wends its way towards the rodent, while the rat, apparently entranced by its own impending death, can only crouch, trembling, as the snake draws nearer. More and more of the snake glides from the bracken until she sees it is probably more than a metre long, and faintly striped. Meredith has never seen a snake in the wild before and is amazed at its effortless movement, how other-worldly it seems. She is about to say something to this effect when the snake pauses, its head flattened and hovering in the air. Eyes like black and gleaming seeds, dull shine of scales. After several seconds of intense concentration, as if tightening the spring of its will, it strikes. There is a flurry of movement, some repulsive thrashing, a little, heartbreaking squeak. Then silence. Meredith peers once more through the gloom, catches a glimpse of a tail flickering before it retracts into the greater, far more complicated, darkness of the bracken.

It's a moment before she is able to speak. 'Jesus Christ,' she says, drinking off the last of her wine.

'Tiger snake,' Jason says, clearly pleased by her response. 'Drought brings them in. Creek's totally dry. He's been there all summer.'

'Is it dangerous?'

'God, yeah. Don't want to get bitten by this fella. You'll be dead in half an hour, I reckon. But he won't come out. I think he's pretty happy in there. Got his water, bit of food. They're quite territorial. As long as you don't go in the pool you'll be all right. Pretty cool, huh?'

Meredith glances at Jason, who has balled up his empty sack. 'Did you catch that rat specially for the snake?'

'Yep. Made my own trap and everything. I get one every week or two.'

'And you've been – what? – *feeding* it?'

'Yep.'

A prickle rises along her bare arms. And she has to admit that, yes, it *is* actually pretty cool.

There is movement in the corner of her eye and Meredith swivels in time to see another boy – the one who was with Jason on the night she first saw him – step out from the tangle of bougainvillea along the side of the property. He's got a fishing rod in one hand and a red fishing box in the other. Shit, she thinks. Shit shit shit.

'What are you guys doing?' the kid says.

Meredith is dumbstruck, but Jason stands to face the other kid. 'Nothing,' he says. 'Wondering about cleaning out the pool, that's all.'

The new kid doesn't approach. 'I thought we were going fishing tonight,' he says, raising the rod.

The Deep End

'Oh,' Jason says. 'Yeah. Um.' And he runs a hand through his hair, this gesture that already she adores.

Meredith steps forward. 'I asked Jason to help me with something.'

The kid looks at her, seems to spend a long time taking her in. Young face still – one of those men who'll have a boyish, wounded face until he's thirty-five, forever hurt that his girlfriend refuses to dress like a hooker in the bedroom; it's the expression, she thinks, of a budding politician.

'How long have you been hiding there?' she asks the kid.

'I wasn't hiding.'

'What have you seen?'

The boy glances at Jason, then back to her. A smirk. 'Nothing.'

Panic rises in her. 'Why are you smiling?'

Then the kid gestures at her with his fishing rod. 'Wait a sec. What's that? On your wrist.' He steps closer. 'That looks like a bracelet my mum lost.'

Meredith holds up her right hand. 'This?'

'Where'd you get that?'

She glances at Jason, whose face is a picture of guilt. 'I bought it, of course. In the city.'

But the boy keeps peering at her wrist. Meredith steps backwards, almost trips on a piece of broken paving.

Finally the boy turns to Jason. '*You* took it, didn't you?'

Jason shakes his head and scoffs, but not convincingly. The scrunched-up canvas sack is in one hand and he's whipping the loose cord against his leg. Lying, for sure.

And the other kid senses it, and Meredith can tell he's becoming swayed by his own theory. She can almost see it firming in his tiny mind as he moves towards Jason. 'My mum reckoned you were a scumbag,' he says.

'That's enough,' says Meredith.

'And she was right. You took it, didn't you? You stole it.'

Jason backs away. 'Fuck off.'

'That's *enough*, I said!' The two boys watch as she places the empty wine glass on the outdoor table and unclasps the bracelet from her wrist. 'What's your name?' Using her schoolteacher's voice now.

'Oscar.'

She holds up the bracelet. 'You really think this belongs to your mum, Oscar?'

'Yes.'

'Then here you go,' she says and she tosses the bracelet towards him. The boy, Oscar, is several metres away, on the other side of the empty pool.

She's never been particularly adept at throwing things – calculations of distance, degrees of heft required – but she knows the instant she releases the bracelet that her instinct, on this occasion, is perfect. The bracelet loops, tangles in midair and falls just short of Oscar, who is standing with mouth agape, both hands full, helplessly watching. The bracelet slithers down the side of the pool with a pleasing *chinkling* sound and comes to rest amid the swampy leaves at the deep end.

'Damn. Sorry about that,' she says.

And all three of them stare at the bracelet which, in the

falling light, seems to be kilometres away, glinting like a distant galaxy. Oscar looks forlorn.

'You'd better jump in and get it,' says Jason after a moment.

'Yes,' she says. 'Quickly now. Before it gets too dark.'

The Shed

1

I STILL CAN'T believe how quickly he took over, or how he did it. Incredible how the inevitable is hardly ever obvious. I found him one afternoon in the shed at the bottom of the garden. It was midwinter, June or July. It was cold and wet. I remember the thick smell of damp earth. The clouds hovered low and it was dark by 4 pm. I don't know how long he had been there – it may have been years. I wasn't really afraid of him, although of course I should have been.

The wife was gone by this time. Packed up some weeks before and wandered off into the sunset. Told me I'd had my chances. Told me she was unhappy. Told me it was the end. The usual things women tell you.

2

I confess that I was drinking at this stage and the house was falling to pieces bit by bit. The kitchen was in ruins, cluttered with pans and plates and takeaway containers. The lounge room was vanishing beneath mountains of unread newspapers and biscuit wrappers. The foul air in the bathroom had begun to take on a life of its own. There was a pile of dry shit in the hallway, which was odd because I had never owned a dog and couldn't even remember one being in the house. Some windows were broken and somebody – perhaps it was me – had covered the spaces with cardboard that fluttered when it was windy. It was a large two-storey house but it smelled suddenly small, like a mangy cupboard.

The only place to be at times like these was in bed. I retreated from the rubbish and mayhem, room by room, until the bedroom that overlooked the backyard was the only vaguely habitable space. I climbed aboard the large, soft bed and hung on like it was a raft of some sort floating above the swell of bottles and butts and broken things.

And you can pretty much do everything you need to in bed: eat, sleep, dream, stare at the ceiling and jerk off to your heart's content. The television sat on a milk crate at the foot of the bed and at my right hand was a chair on which was scattered an assortment of reading material and odds and ends. And, of course, in bed one can drink.

And drinking – and I mean real drinking – is pretty much a full-time occupation. It's not only a glass of wine here and there, the odd long-neck after lunch. It's true that drinkers are disorganised and irresponsible and unreliable, but that's only concerning things other than drinking. A drinker might forget his daughter's birthday or be incapable of managing laundry, but his mind is crystalline when it comes to locating booze. When he needs to call in a three-year-old debt of twenty dollars or remember the Monday night opening hours of a bottle shop on the far side of town.

When drinking, there is planning to be done, things to be considered, decisions to be made. Total destruction takes precision and concentration. It's not as haphazard as it looks. You can't buy takeaway alcohol easily at 4 am, for example, so one needs to be careful of running out at such an inconvenient time. Far better to run dry early in the morning – but not so early as to be caught empty-handed too long before business hours – so all that's required is a short trip to the pub down the road for your morning cask of wine. Drinking is not a social event, it's an interior monologue. God forbid you should ever have to sit with others to get it done. Doing it is only half the work. There's thinking about doing it as well. It all takes time.

3

I can't even remember why I went down to the shed in the first place. Probably looking for something to pawn or scrounging for empty bottles to sell. The only light was that of the late afternoon coming through the open door. Everything looked grey and furry. One wall bore the drawn shapes of garden tools, like the crime-scene outlines of murder victims.

Grass was growing through the floor and vines curled between gaps in the walls. A light rain grizzled on the tin roof like an army of tiny feet. The shed smelled like all garden sheds, of dirt and oil and the bitter tang of fertiliser.

But there was something else. I was surprised to detect my own sharp smell, perhaps drawn out by the rain I'd staggered through to reach the shed. It was the machinery of my body, working vainly to expel the toxins I was pouring into it. I sniffed my armpits and yanked a handful of wet hair in front of my nose, but I was inured to myself. The smell was of something different, something muddy and fecund.

I stepped further into the gloom. An ancient handmower rested against a wheelbarrow; small packets of seeds were arranged on a wooden rack designed for the purpose. The desiccated remains of failed gardening enterprises. A battered paper kite hung in one corner.

I trailed some fingers across a dusty cardboard box of papers and books and reached out idly to caress a thick, squat roll of brown carpet standing on its end in the middle of the floor. To my surprise, it was not only wet but warm as well. It moaned and turned around heavily. I found myself staring into a pair of dark, apelike eyes, framed by dank hair.

By now the rain had stopped. There were just the sounds and smells of our breathing.

4

He sat in the kitchen, naked and wet. A grey puddle formed on the floor beneath his chair. The long hair covering his entire body was flat and black against his shiny, pink skin. He didn't seem afraid, and made no sound apart from the occasional low groan, which may have been of distress or satisfaction, it was hard to tell.

He sat with his round shoulders hunched and hands clasped loosely upon his lean and hairy knees. Although his bearing changed very little, those large, sooty eyes circled ceaselessly and took in the entire room. It was difficult to know what he knew. He took no interest in the tin of baked beans open on the table in front of him, although his nostrils flared slightly when it was first set down. By now it was night. There was only the two of us. The back door and kitchen windows were all open wide to rid the house of his stench, one I could feel on my skin.

I was drinking from a bottle of sherry and eating chips from the local fish and chip shop, popping them into my mouth one by one. They were barely warm, like the small, narrow corpses of recently murdered things. I sat watching him on the opposite side of the table. Despite his hairy, unwieldy torso and barnyard eyes, he looked like a man. He breathed like a machine, deep and even.

5

He was still there two days later, but no drier. His wetness was apparently something that seeped from his pink skin. The puddle on the floor expanded and trickled away beneath the kitchen door. As far as I could tell, he had barely moved. I waved a hand in front of his eyes, held up a piece of toast to his dark lips. When I tried to scare him by clapping my hands or banging two old cooking pots together, he just angled his head away and screwed up his round face a little. His body made a sticky sound when he moved.

'What are you, then?' I asked. His unresponsiveness was getting to me. 'What are you? Are you human? You stink like a fucking animal. You know that? You really stink.'

He sort of looked at me with his watery, brown eyes and let out a rumbling groan, not of anger or frustration, but something darker and far more terrible. The sound vibrated in the air. I lit a cigarette and watched him. Smoke filled the small space between us. I drank.

6

Sometime later, the following day or week, he was gone from the kitchen. I wondered if I had imagined the entire thing, but on the floor was a shallow puddle. Closer inspection revealed several clods of long, black hair. I looked through the grimy window into the garden. It was still raining. The shed door was still open. I imagined him snuffling around in there with his long, articulate fingers and liquid eyes. I would wait until the rain stopped and the place had dried out and then I would close the shed door and set fire to it, with him inside. I could wait. What else was I going to do?

It was only late morning and already I was in ruins. I checked my alcohol supplies and was relieved to discover an unopened cask of wine and half a bottle of port that I had forgotten buying. I made a quick calculation. If today was

The Shed

Friday, then tomorrow was Saturday, which meant I could still buy something locally until late if I needed to. Perfect.

I cut the mouldy corners from some bread to make toast and even managed to find some coffee on the laminated bench under the window. The wife must have bought it before she left. I was suddenly, inexplicably, in good spirits. I ate my breakfast, shaved off several weeks' worth of thick beard and stood in the kitchen doorway to smoke a cigarette. Rainwater fell from the gutters and eaves like a trembling curtain. God knows why, but the world seemed full of possibility.

There comes a brief moment in every bender when you're able to see things for what they are – not just what you construct in order to be able to keep drinking – and this was that moment. It is always frightening. I saw the tatty garden dotted with empty bottles and cans, the sink full of broken, mouldy dishes. I saw the stains on the walls and the wreckage of furniture, the cold skulking in the sharpest corners of the house. I held a hand in front of my face. It was like a foreign object, the nails ragged and worn, like something you'd use to dig in the dirt.

I flicked my cigarette butt into the garden and went back inside. Okay. It was time to clean the place up, to try to get things together again. I walked into the lounge room. It was dim and musty. I opened the curtains and window and there he was, sitting on the low couch with those hands, as always, clasped gently between his knees. He looked up at me with a look of something like embarrassment and it was like the first time, just the sounds of our breathing in that small, enclosed space. We looked at each other. 'What are you doing?' I yelled. *'What are you doing?'*

He didn't answer, of course. Made no sign he'd even understood. And then slowly, very deliberately, I picked up the telephone. I was going to call the police, call someone, the local loony bin or something and get them to come and take this thing away, this thing that had taken up residence in my house. In my house. He watched me with those begging eyes as I did it, as I raised the plastic receiver to my ear. And I watched him watching me, so he knew exactly what was happening, but when I put the receiver to my ear, there was no tone, no sound of any sort, only the humming silence of an unpaid bill.

The moment, it seemed, had passed.

7

I woke up at some point in the day and waited. The bed smelled grey. Even from behind closed eyes, I could sense something was different but I was reluctant to find out what it could be. Whatever it was could wait. Things had moved beyond the point where I could reasonably expect them to improve. I could hear birds outside and the sighing of wind through trees.

When I opened my eyes, it was no surprise, really. His dark eyes staring down at me. His body was still wet, and dripped slightly, although the terrible smell was gone. Either that, or I had become accustomed to it. We stared at each other for a long time, me lying on my back under a thin doona, while he stood slack-shouldered at the end of the bed. I'm sure we could have stayed like that forever, trading blinks, waiting for something to happen.

After some time I pushed the doona aside and swung around to put my feet on the cold, rough carpet. He stayed utterly still while I moved around the room and pulled on some clothes, although I knew that in the time I took to stagger down the hall and through the front door onto the street, he had lumbered into my bed and eased himself beneath my covers.

Theories of Relativity

I'M ELEVEN YEARS old. Our father fills the bath with cold water, orders me to dump a tray of ice cubes into it and tells my older brother Anthony to strip off his clothes. Our father is tall, angular and taciturn, a man accustomed to being obeyed by his family, if no one else. His crucial error is to mistake our disdain for respect. He has a stopwatch in one hand. 'We'll see what you're made of,' he sniffs.

I stand in the dim hallway looking up at him, listening intently to his instructions; I know they will be issued once only and I risk a clip over the ear if I ask him to repeat them. Our little sister Janet lingers in a doorway with a strand of hair in her mouth, staring, like always. She's nine. Our mother is out somewhere. My brother's face is grim but stoic as he realises what is about to happen. It is midwinter. Rain is drumming on the roof. It dawns on me that I will remember this afternoon for the rest of my life.

Our father is adamant that Anthony and I be toughened up and has devised a variety of techniques to ensure we will never be in the slightest bit girly. When we play soccer in the backyard, for instance, he never allows us to win because that doesn't happen in the real world. He refuses to help us up if we fall down ('Self-inflicted. No crying. Stand up little man'). Years earlier – and this is embarrassing – I faltered one cold night in my toilet training and our father took me outside, yanked off my pyjamas and hosed me down as a method of instruction.

Our father doesn't drink, doesn't smoke and thinks those who do are damn fools. He has no time for sentimentality and the few jokes he utters are usually at someone else's expense. The world is a harsh place and it's his job to equip his sons the best way he knows how. After all, it was good enough for him; we could do a lot worse than turn out like he did. Little does he know exactly what this will entail.

The bath test and the toilet training and so on happen before the accident, of course. Afterwards, he wouldn't have dared.

It seemed everyone changed in the months after our father's accident, or that the entire family was reorganised in a way that was never clear to me. I felt I had lived through a revolution, say, or a natural disaster, whereby everything had become different, but in ways too seismic to pinpoint. Our mother took up smoking, for a start, and became dry-witted and elegant. She began to say things like: *Oh, that's marvellous* or *Sweetie, please don't do that, I have a headache,* while sitting on the couch in the afternoon, flicking through a glossy magazine. Indeed, it seemed our mother had barely existed until the moment of our father's accident. Even her name, Kate, which had seemed rather pedestrian before, assumed a more cinematic quality. She started wearing lipstick around the house and having afternoon 'kips', a concept she had picked up from an American magazine. At first – in addition to everything else that had happened – it was somewhat disconcerting, but Anthony and I both came to like this new persona. She became the type of parent the other kids probably talked about at home with their own, more mundane families; ours was a low-grade, schoolyard celebrity, like the Cambodian kid at school whose brother had been shot by communists.

People admired our mother when she came to pick Anthony and me up from school. She had fallen pregnant with my brother when she was seventeen and so was only thirty-one years old at that time, even though our father was ten years older. She was still attractive and the other fathers paid her quite a bit of attention. I didn't mind, but Anthony became furious if she flirted too long with Mr Jacobs and he would refuse to speak to her after we returned home. When this happened, our mother would expend considerable effort coaxing him from the cave of his mood, fetching treats from the pantry and swearing to behave herself in future. *Come on, darling. There! Have an Iced VoVo.*

Anthony changed as well. He emerged from the night of the accident into another, more restless person. He was fourteen, so he was hardly old, but now he declined to accompany me around the neighbourhood to see whose fruit trees we might climb. No more hide and seek. He even took to calling our mother Kate, rather than Mother or Mum, a practice she did nothing to discourage, even though our father disapproved.

Anthony was taller than me, more athletic, much better looking, and possessed a roguish charm that attracted the type of girl willing to do things nice girls were not. He played guitar. He had been born missing the tip of the little finger on his left hand, a disfigurement that only heightened his appeal rather than diminished it, as it might have done in other boys. My brother also had a competitive streak that prohibited him from gaining any real pleasure from his success with girls or sport. He could be cruel, as I knew only too well: he forgot people's names on purpose; he mimicked them mercilessly behind their backs; he told vicious jokes about neighbours and classmates; he had long called me Mr Einstein, on account of my interest in the great physicist's theories of time and space.

We still shared a room and I would lie awake and stare at his sleeping profile, hoping to detect a clue to his sudden alteration. After all, it wasn't like the accident had befallen *him*. Sometimes he prowled through the house at night and occasionally even slept elsewhere, on the couch in the living room or on the daybed in our father's study. On the single instance I crept after him, he turned in the hallway, pressed a hand to my chest and shook his head in such a way that dissuaded me from following him ever again. 'Back off, Mr Einstein,' he hissed.

*

Our father was a captain in the army. Before the accident, he liked to talk authoritatively at barbecues about immigration policy and 'covert actions' in South-East Asia as if he were privy to secret information, but he merely shuffled bits of paper from one office to the next and overheard rumours in the canteen along with everyone else who worked in his building. He had joined the army with the boyish hope of being sent overseas to some exotic war zone to battle terrorists or communists but had never been closer to genuine military action than manoeuvres in Darwin one year (the highlight of his entire life), and he certainly wouldn't be deployed now, considering his age – not to mention the injury.

His own father, our grandfather, had been in the army and had been bitter about being sent away to shoot people in Vietnam; our father was bitter that he never had the opportunity to shoot at anyone. He was merely a public servant with a fancy uniform. If asked about his foot injury, he mumbled something about a 'hunting mishap', which was true, I suppose. Naturally, the accident changed our father most of all.

The morning of the accident was wet and frosty. I heard our father moving about in the bathroom next door. Anthony slept in his bed on the other side of our room, blissfully unaware until our father burst in and roused each of us with a slap to the side of our heads. 'Come on, lads,' he said. 'We move out in ten minutes.'

The car interior was almost as cold as it was outside. Our father didn't believe in excessive comfort. Besides, we were rugged up. We were going hunting; there was no point getting too cosy. In the back seat, I breathed on the glass and drew a face in the damp, silvery fog. The rising sun flickered behind trees.

Our father had been promising to take us hunting for some time but my excitement at the prospect of shooting a real rifle was tempered with guilt. Our mother thought we were too young for such an expedition and she didn't approve of shooting animals for sport – objections our father overruled.

'My old man used to take me out here when I was about your age,' our father was saying to Anthony, who sat beside him in the front seat.

Our father didn't usually speak unless necessary, and then in a clipped manner that suggested he was keen to be done with it as soon as he had made his point. But now I recognised in his voice the tone he reserved for speeches on The State Of The Economy, The Difference Between Men And Women or How To Tell The ABC Has Been Overrun By Lefties.

From the back seat I could see my brother's face in profile. Anthony was weirdly lit in the alien glow from the dashboard lights so that his skin appeared dusted with green phosphorescence. A crescent-shaped scar was visible on his right cheek where he had fallen during a game of chasey years earlier. Anthony inclined his head to show he was listening. I knew he hated these little homilies but endured them with the same stoicism he marshalled for the occasional strapping across the leg. He was a serious boy, introspective, given to harbouring grudges – none of which I really knew, or knew only vaguely, on this cold morning. I loved and admired my brother even though he intimidated me because it seemed that, should it ever become necessary, he would get by very well without any of us, myself included.

Our father changed gears and slowed the car to cross a railway line. 'You never really knew your grandfather, but he was a great man. Really, a great man.' The car bobbled over the tracks. 'I loved those trips. Me and him. The *men*, you know. Course we used to eat the rabbits. Take them home for Mum to cook. Made nice stews, she did.'

I listened over the thrum of the car's engine. Although directed at Anthony, I knew our father's speeches were intended for anyone in earshot. My own memories of our grandfather were vague: a grizzled muzzle; the smell of urine; a flap of grey, greasy hair pasted across his forehead. Anthony and I were both a little fearful of the late widower, who had lived nearby and visited every few days to have dinner and watch television. Although our father had often extolled his virtues and urged us to respect him, neither Anthony nor I had ever felt comfortable with him and avoided being alone with him. When he died a year earlier, our mother told us – as she told all family members and visitors – not to mention our grandfather's name in our father's presence in case we upset him.

'When I was your age,' our father was saying, 'we used to lay traps. Caught a wild dog once. Stupid thing. Those traps were hard to set. Always a chance of getting snagged . . .'

I stopped listening and wiped my bleary window clean with the sleeve of my duffel coat. My nose ran with the cold. I thought of my warm bed, and of our mother, who would by now be standing at the kitchen window in her dressing-gown, drinking tea with the serious expression she adopted for her morning ritual. Janet would be playing with her teddy on the lounge room floor. The image prompted in me a flood of wild, helpless love and suddenly I wished I were at home with them instead of sitting in this freezing car. A kookaburra on a wire fence watched us pass.

'. . . and I guess,' our father was saying when I tuned in again, 'I guess that the thing I would hope for us – for you boys and me – is you would respect me like I respected my father. That's why sometimes I'm hard on you. That's all. It's for your own good, you know.'

It was the most personal speech I had ever heard him make and I was amazed and almost terrified to detect a quaver of emotion in his voice. Neither Anthony nor I said anything but my brother reached a hand over and patted our father gently on the shoulder. 'It's okay,' he said, and turned to me in the back seat. 'We understand, don't we, Nick?' I mumbled agreement. For the next hour we drove in companionable silence, as if we had used all the words allocated us for the morning.

We arrived at an isolated car park at around 9 am and piled out of the car. We unloaded the rifles and knapsacks and set out for the camp site, which was two kilometres across a grassy stretch of bushland. The frosty grass crunched beneath our boots and our hot exhalations billowed around us in the glinting morning sunlight. Small birds darted about in the high grass. I felt anxious, as if my body were aware of something hidden from the more articulate parts of myself, but perhaps this is just how I remember it.

Ten years later I woke in the afternoon heat and slid from the couch. Richie Benaud was calling the cricket in a droning voice that sounded like a small plane perpetually losing altitude. It was hot and I had staggered over to the couch and fallen asleep after the Sunday roast our mother organised every few weeks. I was twenty-one that summer, in many ways still an innocent. I had started going out with a pleasant, bovine girl called Julie who did deliveries for the bike shop where I worked on weekends. I had by this time moved out of home and was undertaking a degree in physics, but Anthony stayed on while he tried to be a rock star. The lunches were always desultory affairs peppered with small talk, and afterwards each of us dissolved into different parts of the house.

Half asleep, I followed murmuring voices and found my mother and Anthony huddled at the study window, watching our father as he limped across the lawn doing odd jobs in the garden. Our father didn't know he was being observed, just as Anthony and Mother were unaware of me standing in the doorway to the darkened study. As they so often did, they were giggling at a private joke.

Although he was only twenty-three, two years older than me, Anthony seemed to live in a whole other world, to which our mother had access. At that moment she had a cigarette in her right hand and she turned her face away from Anthony and exhaled the grey smoke up into the study's cool corners. It reminded me of a conical plume sprayed from a can of insect repellent.

'*Look* at him,' she was saying, referring to our father as he struggled to raise himself from where he had been kneeling to weed a garden bed. 'An old man in a dry month.' She had been drinking wine at lunch.

My brother didn't say anything. She offered him her cigarette. He took it casually, barely noticing, drew on it and handed it back. I had never before seen my brother smoke a cigarette. It shocked me.

'Do you ever regret what happened?' our mother asked Anthony.

He shook his head. He exhaled his cigarette smoke and looked at our mother as if something had occurred to him. 'Why? Do you?'

Mother rested her head on Anthony's shoulder and laughed. 'Hardly, darling. *Hardly.*'

I wasn't exactly sure what I had just witnessed, but it felt indecent. It brought to mind the dismal thrill Robert Oppenheimer must have felt when he discovered the technology for the Bomb. When I had composed myself I eased away from the study door, crept down the hallway to the lounge room, gathered my jacket and bag and left without saying goodbye to anyone. Long after the gnashing implements should have been out of earshot, I detected the *snip snip snip* of garden shears as our father hobbled about the backyard.

*

Our father tells Anthony the cold water is excellent for his circulation. He smiles his smile that shows no teeth. 'It's only *three minutes*. You don't even have to put your head under, like when I had to do it.'

I watch Anthony take off his clothes. He goes about it slowly, as if memorising each movement for later use. He leaves his watch on. The watch belonged to our grandfather – he acquired it in Vietnam – and he gave it to Anthony not long before he died, much to our father's chagrin. Our father said our grandfather was half blind and demented at the end. *He only gave it to you because he thought you were me*, he would say, a comment guaranteed to rile Anthony almost more than anything else.

Finally, when my brother is naked, skin puckered, shivering, he walks down the hallway into the bathroom and steps gingerly into the bath, drawing a sharp breath as he does so.

I found it almost impossible to return to the family home after that summer afternoon. Every few months my mother would ring to urge my attendance at lunch, but I always found a reason not to go – I had a report due, I was going to Wilsons Promontory with Julie, I was tired after a night out at the pub with my mates.

'Oh, come on, sweetie,' Mother would slur down the phone line. 'You know your brother would love to see you. And we *always love* to have that Julie around the house.'

Only my mother could so effortlessly squeeze two lies into such a short speech. The thought of kissing her lips made me queasy. The thought of seeing Anthony made me furious. The thought of seeing our father made me feel, strangely enough, almost unbearably sad.

After we had been tramping for an hour or so through thick bush, our father stopped and threw up a hand for my brother and me to halt. My heart began thumping. My mouth dried up. Were we actually going to shoot something? Anthony hefted his rifle. I followed suit. Our father crouched and peered into the undergrowth. Then he turned to us and mouthed the word *pig*. A pig? A wild pig. Now that *would* be something. Our father had told us how unlikely it would be to come across a pig but said rabbits would be fine for our first hunting expedition. 'Nothing wrong with shooting little bunnies,' he said. 'It's still hunting after all.'

Our father shuffled backwards and indicated for us to do the same. He looked scared. Anthony smirked. Presently, I saw something move about in the thick bushes. My heart was really pounding and my palms were moist. Again I thought of our mother and Janet, safe at home, eating crumpets with honey. There came a snuffling noise and my father raised his rifle; what lumbered from the bushes was not a pig at all, but a huge wombat. Anthony cheered the creature's entrance. The wombat – which was the size of a short-legged, obese dog – looked around for a moment and waddled off into the bushes. I thought it was cute, but our father was displeased. He gave us a stern look, as if it were our fault.

We trudged all over the countryside but didn't have much luck that day. 'It takes a while,' our father said, 'to get your eye in, to be able to spot things moving about and realise what they might be.'

Night fell quickly and we returned to our camp. We heated a chicken stew our mother had prepared. Our father hummed to himself as he ladled out the dinner and fiddled with the fire. He seemed possessed of a sense of wellbeing I didn't recall observing before.

Before we turned in for the night, he got up and muttered something about going to the toilet, and began picking his way into the darkness with the torch.

'You should go that way,' Anthony said, pointing in the opposite direction. 'There's a clearing through there. It's easier to find your way.'

Our father turned and stood still, as if Anthony had said something quite unusual. He looked at both of us, his face animated by the light from the flickering fire. At that moment he appeared wholly unfamiliar to me, like a stranger emerged from the bush. 'Okay,' he said at last. 'Good man.' And he set off the way Anthony had indicated, ruffling my brother's hair as he went past.

The tree trunks trembled and twitched in the campfire light. My cheeks blazed from its heat. I was exhausted from the early morning drive and the endless tramping through bushland. Hunting wasn't as fun as I had thought it would be, and we still had an entire day left. Anthony threw wood onto the fire.

Then an awful scream.

*

Even at the age of thirteen, my brother is genuinely tough. Not in a show-offish way, but you can sense it about him, and it is perhaps this quality that drives our father to devise ever more rigorous tests. With a hand on each side of the tub for balance, Anthony lowers himself into the freezing water. The ice cubes joggle about his knees and chest. I can see he is suffering but my father won't activate the stopwatch until Anthony is fully immersed. Eventually, my brother takes a deep breath and lies back with his hands across his chest. I feel humiliated on his behalf as his penis shrivels to the size of a witchetty grub and his nipples turn licorice-coloured. Janet sidles away. Our father clicks the stopwatch. 'Okay. We are . . . *Go!*'

It took Anthony and me only a minute to locate our father. He was lying on his back in a ditch. His eyes were clenched shut and his mouth set in a grimace of pain. 'Get it off!' he was saying. 'Get it *off!* Get it *off!*' His torch was on the ground nearby. Anthony picked it up and played the light over his face and down the length of his body. Our father's ankle was clamped in a steel rabbit trap. His trousers were torn. There was thick blood, a flap of purple flesh. I squatted at his side, but my brother yanked me back so hard that I fell to the damp ground. Our father was by this time writhing in agony, pounding at the damp earth with a fist. 'Quick! Pull the latch, Anthony. Pull . . . the bloody . . . thing . . . back. *Quick! Get it off me!*'

*

Theories of Relativity

When Anthony's three minutes in the cold water are up, our father says: 'Well done, little man. Out you get. Nick, fetch his towel.'

But Anthony doesn't move, doesn't say a word. He doesn't even open his eyes. All he does is lift a hand from the water to *scratch his nose*, as if he were on the couch in front of the TV. Again our father tells him to come out but Anthony won't listen and he ends up staying in that bath for ages – maybe half an hour – until our mother comes back and asks what in the hell is going on. She is furious. By this time my brother's entire body is the colour of a fresh bruise. His lips are grey. Our father has stormed off and Janet is slumped in the hallway crying. I help our mother lift Anthony out. He is shaking hard and he can barely walk, but his half-lit smile is the same one that will resurface the night of the accident, when he squats down leisurely beside our screaming father, draws up the sleeve of his jacket to reveal his watch and says: 'Okay. Let's see what you're made of. On my signal . . . Three minutes from . . . *Now!*'

What the Darkness Said

WHEN I WAS about five years old, still entangled in childhood, my mother fell pregnant. All through autumn she swelled, until by winter she was as big as a house and the shape of a capital B. My father laughed his toothy laugh when he touched her belly and told me she must have swallowed a pumpkin seed. My mother batted his hands away and smiled. At night she pulled me close and let me listen to her smooth, rounded belly. It sounded like outer space and I imagined my brother adrift upon its vast emptinesses, hanging on grimly until the time when he would land in our family. I waited long and hard for my little brother.

My new brother would sleep in my room. Lying in bed at night I conjured his still-unborn face from the darkness and held lengthy conversations with him. I imagined the things we would be able to do when he was ready. We would play games and go on secret adventures in the bush with a compass and map, the way I had done with my father.

I would show him where the old goanna lived and the best way to build a cubby house. There would be an entire lifetime of things to do.

When he was finally born, I discovered his name was Martin. He was small and wrinkled. He cried a lot and snuffled in his sleep. I lugged him from room to room. Together we watched my mother pulling rhubarb and herbs from her sunny garden.

When he was about two, Martin learned to say my name. *Alex*, he shrieked. *Alex*. Later, I took him down to the creek at the edge of our small property with our dog, Bailey. We crouched in the grass to see the bunyip that drank there late in the afternoons. We tried to catch a frog but Bailey scared him away. I showed Martin the birds and we squatted on the ground to watch the bull ants going about their business. His childish breath scattered the dry dirt and caused the ants to stop what they were doing and wave their antennae around angrily in the air like fists. He loved apples and pears. He loved the sound when I blew a raspberry.

Because I spent so much time with him, I was often the only one who could understand Martin's babble. My parents would call me in to translate.

'Alex. What's Martin saying?' they would ask.

'He's saying that we saw a bunyip down at the creek.'

'Oh, really. That's lucky, sweetheart. Not everyone sees a bunyip, you know. What was he doing?'

'He said the bunyip was drinking some water.'

'Was he a big bunyip?'

'Not really. He said it was the usual size.'

'Oh, I see. Well, you be careful down there. Don't go in the water.'

'Yeah. We know.'

'Are you ready for dinner? Hush, Bailey. Outside!'

'Yeah. We're ready. But Martin says he wants ice-cream.'

'I see.'

When he was four, my brother disappeared while we were at the market with my mother buying vegetables. He had been holding my hand and slipped away in the crowd. We searched everywhere. Nobody knew where he was for three days. I imagined him tramping through the bush on his stumpy legs, humming one of the songs I'd taught him, naming the trees in his burbling voice as he went, saying, *Hello dragonflies, hello kookaburra, how are you?* The police searched everywhere but he was probably in that muddy drain where that man had stuffed him the whole time.

A few days later they put Martin in a box and lowered him into a grave. A family of cockatoos screeched in a nearby tree. The soil was hard and crumbly and I worried about how he would breathe. I thought perhaps that we should put some fruit in the grave or else he might get hungry, but no one paid me any attention.

Nobody talked much about Martin after that. Nobody talked about anything. For a while at school the kids and teachers stayed away. My parents said it wasn't my fault. My father used to say we lost him, as if that was the problem, but I think finding him in that drain with no clothes on was worse.

'He was Wednesday's child,' my mother said. And she went to her room and climbed into bed, where she stayed for a long time. She said she wouldn't come out again until they caught the sick bastard that did those things to Martin. My father stood on the verandah and rolled cigarettes, one after another, until there was a pile of them unsmoked at his feet. Sometimes at night I heard whimpering in the yard but it was only a piece of tin from the shed flapping in the hot, dark wind.

I was in grade five. We learned about bushfires and the names of all the oceans: Pacific, Atlantic, Southern. I had never seen an ocean. It seemed impossible to me for so much water to be in the same place at the same time. The creek at the bottom of our property only ran in spring. In summer it was just a ditch of blackberry.

One day during a dry lunchtime, some kids were talking about the old Norton place on the edge of town. Samantha Riley said a witch lived there and most of the other kids said so too.

'Yeah. She comes around the town at night, when everyone is asleep.'

'My mum says that's not true.'

'It *is* true.'

'How do you know?'

'Because my brother *saw* her.'

'He can't, stupid. Only dogs can see her. That's why they bark at night for no reason. When they see her.'

'She has a snake with a tongue made of flames.'

'*Blue* flames.'
'Yeah.'
'She smokes a pipe.'
'She's *black*.'
'Yeah. An Abo.'
'And eats herbs and things.'
'*Yeah.*'

We were near the wooden shelter shed, beneath the shade of the huge old gum tree that swayed like a grandparent. The schoolyard smelled of eucalypt, dust and orange peel. George Langton was handballing a footy up and down in the air. It was far too hot to play anything, even cricket. Cicadas droned.

Then Samantha Riley brushed her damp, blonde hair out of her eyes and leaned in close. She had a smear of Vegemite on her lower lip. 'You know what else?' she asked in a whisper.

'What?'
'She makes babies out there.'
'She does not.'
'*Does.*'
'Yes. She does. She makes the mummy drink tea –'
'Penny tea.'
'That's right. Pennyroll tea. The mummy waits there for a while then the witch plants something in the garden out the back of her place and babies grow there.'
'Like bulbs.'
'She plants baby bulbs.'
'Yeah. It's obvious, really.'

'Yeah. Obvious. You go out there and pick yours.'

'Sometimes it takes a whole day.'

'She knows all sorts of things.'

I imagined a tree of babies, each dangling at the end of a spindly limb, mewling, waiting to be plucked by parents-to-be. I imagined Martin's scrunched-up face, the way he jammed his tiny fist against his wet mouth when he was newly born. I thought of my mother, still under her covers, and my father on the verandah, each waiting, it seemed, for Martin to return and barely able to move until he did so.

The bell rang for the end of lunch and as I was running inside the idea came to me fully formed, like an egg.

The old Norton place was at the end of Chinaman's Track, according to Samantha Riley, who seemed to know everything about the witch except her name. You followed the river for a bit and it was just there. A few hours' walk. 'You can't tell anyone, but my sister went there last year,' she told me. 'But she didn't find any she liked, so she came back empty. Now she has to stay at home on weekends.'

One Saturday afternoon I packed a bag with fruit and water and took some money from the flour tin. I told my mother and father I was going to visit my friend Simon who lived down the road. They nodded and off I went. I wanted to explain where I was going, but thought it would be better to surprise them.

It was hot and there was smoke in the air from a fire at Ginger Gully. *Hot as buggery*, my father would have said. The air thrummed with insects and heat. I could hear

What the Darkness Said

Mr Sutton clearing his land with a chainsaw. I followed Chinaman's Track past the abandoned mine shafts and up the hill. The bushland was different here. Around our place it was green, especially with my mother's vegie patch and the willow trees around the creek. I had never been this far by myself before. It was like another country. The trees were twisted, as if straining to break out of the stony ground. My shoe dug into my right heel and I could already feel a blister forming. Other trees scratched my legs. What if a bushfire came through here? They said you sometimes didn't even know until it was too late. Dingoes ran right through the flames and out the other side; trees exploded.

When I got to the top of the hill I had sweat running all down my face and I couldn't even see the river yet. I was already tired. There were just more trees and a bruise of dark smoke on the horizon. That trembling heat. A bull ant bit me on the knee and it felt like someone had stuck a red-hot pin into my flesh. Tears pressed against the inside of my face until they leaked out through my eyes. I sat on a stump and wept. This was a stupid idea. There was no way I would ever get to the dumb witch's place. Maybe Samantha Riley was wrong after all? The world was much larger than I thought. It seemed to go on forever, to be without end. This was a stupid idea.

Who knows how long I cried for? It seemed a long time but when I was done with my tears, or they were done with me, I drank some water and ate an apple and felt a bit better. The rest of the bush was silent. Even the flies were asleep for once. Then I heard a strange, high-pitched sound. On the ground nearby was a baby bird. It had no feathers. I could see dark veins beneath its papery skin. It opened and closed its beak and scratched in the dry dust.

I leaned down until I was so close I could see its heart fluttering beneath its skin. I wasn't sure if the bird could see me through its milky eyes but it squeaked louder and moved its head around in a circle. Already ants were clambering over its pink and trembling body, shooting in and out of its mouth, right across its eyes, deciding which bits to eat first. Soon the little creature would vanish entirely beneath the black swarm and that would be that. The thought of it made me itchy. Curious and appalled, I watched the little bird squirm in the dirt. I wondered what it could be thinking.

'What's that you've found there?'

Still on my haunches, I spun around in the dirt to see a man standing behind me. He was tall and he wore a hat. I didn't say anything and after a few seconds he leaned down with his hands on his knees. 'Ah,' he said. 'A baby bird.' Then the man looked at me with a serious face. 'What shall we do?'

I wasn't sure if I should be afraid. I shrugged and the man crouched down on one knee to peer at the bird. He was older than my dad, with wrinkles. He smelled of cigarettes and soap. The side of his neck was red from being outside a lot and sweat ran down his face. 'A kookaburra,' he said. 'Perhaps fallen from the nest. That happens sometimes. Nature can be cruel.'

It was late afternoon by this stage. It would be dark in an hour or so. A burnt leaf landed on my shoulder and when I picked it up, it crumbled in my fist.

'Are you out here by yourself?' the man asked.

I nodded.

'Do your parents know?'

I didn't say anything.

He looked at me for a long time and seemed to give all this some thought. 'It isn't really very safe out here today,' he said. 'There's bushfire warnings, you know.'

Still I said nothing, just fiddled in the dirt with a stick. My face was hot and dry. There was a red mark on my knee where the bull ant had bitten me. I felt a long way from anywhere. I wondered if my parents had even noticed I was gone.

'So, what are you doing out here in the bush by yourself, on a sweltering day like this?' the man asked.

I fumbled in my bag, grabbed my bottle and drank some water. I didn't want to tell this stranger anything. I felt foolish. I didn't know what sweltering meant. It would soon be night and nobody knew where I was. Not even I knew where I was.

'I'm sure you weren't looking for abandoned birds,' he said.

'Will it be okay?' The bird, I meant.

The tall stranger leaned down to inspect the creature. 'I don't know. He doesn't look too good. I had a cockatoo once I found on the ground like this one. Took her home and she grew up big and strong. Used to live out the back on a perch I built for her. Called her Fred.'

'But that's a boy's name.'

'Yeah. But I thought at first she was a boy and couldn't think of a better name.'

'What happened to her?'

'Oh, she hung around for about three years, then went off with a flock. Used to come back every so often but I haven't seen her in a while.'

'Don't you miss her?'

'Yes. Sometimes, but she was awfully loud and cranky. Things change. I miss what might have been, more than what was, but I have plenty of other animals. I have enough to do.' The stranger tipped his hat back to scratch his forehead, then looked at me closely. He had very blue eyes. 'You're Martin's brother, aren't you? Alex?'

Martin. That word. I nodded because that was all I could do. Hair fell over my eyes. I couldn't speak for a long time and we sat there among the crackling trees. Then it all came out in a rush. I said I was going to get another baby for my mum and dad, a new brother for me, about the witch, about the tree of babies and how I got lost, and how the bull ant bit me on the knee look at the red bump there now.

He put a hand on my shoulder.

Hot tears ran down my face and plopped onto my dusty knees. 'Do you know where she is?' I asked.

'The witch?'

'Can you take me there? Please. I think she's near here somewhere. I've got money.'

'Who told you about this witch?'

'A girl at school. Samantha Riley.'

What the Darkness Said

The stranger thought about this for a few seconds. 'Riley, eh? I see.'

The bird had started squeaking again, perhaps even more loudly, and tried to lift its bulbous head off the ground. A line of ants trailed from its poor body into the undergrowth. 'Perhaps we should take him home?' the man said.

This seemed an amazing idea.

He pointed down the hill with a long, thin finger. 'My house is nearby. Just down there. Perhaps we should take the bird back there and see if we can save him. What do you think?'

I thought about this for a minute, then nodded and stood up. By now the sky was dark with orange smoke. I blew the ants from the bird's naked body as best I could and the man showed me how to carry it in the fold of my t-shirt. It weighed almost nothing but trembled like an organ against my stomach. The man told me his name was William. He said how hard it was to feed a wild animal, to get them to take food from a human. 'It's quite an art,' he said. I followed him down Chinaman's Track in the bleakening afternoon.

William's house was hidden among thick trees about ten minutes further along the narrow path. I didn't even know it was there until we were nearly inside. Navigating through the cluttered cabin, he turned on some lights. He took the squeaking bird from me and placed it gently in a small, wooden box lined with fabric. I stood near the door, unsure where to go or what I was even doing here. Cats drifted through the shadows, like slow-moving fish. I looked back the way we had come. The path we had taken was vanishing in the darkness. An army of crickets shrilled. Mosquitoes whined past my face.

William moved quickly, gathering things together. He fluttered about his junkyard nest. After a while I crept further into the little house. Inside it was dark and cool and smelled of dried herbs and woodsmoke. 'I need you to help me,' he said.

I stood there without saying a word. What could *I* do?

'Well. Can you help?' he asked again.

I shrugged. I was hungry and wanted to go home. William waited. He seemed patient. 'Yes,' I said at last.

William showed me how to mash some stuff with a mortar and pestle while he went out the back and collected things from his garden. I don't know what he used, or even if he knew what he was doing. It was hard work but I kept on grinding until there was a thick paste. William boiled something on the stove and added it to my mixture.

It took a while to grind the paste properly and I had to change hands a few times, but eventually it was ready and William drew some up in an eye dropper. He handed it to me. 'There you go.'

I stared at the dropper in his stumpy fingers for a long time. His fingernails were all bitten and cracked. He didn't blink. The dropper shook minutely between his thumb and forefinger. One of the cats brushed against my leg. I jumped and William hissed for it to get out. I was afraid, but took the dropper and angled the nozzle against the little bird's beak, my own mouth opening in sympathy as I did so.

What the Darkness Said

The bird's head waved around like a plant in the wind. The poor little thing was obviously desperate but didn't understand how to eat, just sort of opened and closed its mouth randomly. Its tongue flickered and the liquid soaked into the cloth lining the box. It was hot. Sweat dripped down my face and into my mouth. The bird was dying. It was dying.

I don't know how long I crouched over the box, making noises with my mouth, urging the tiny bird to drink. It seemed like hours, most of the night, at least, but finally we managed, this bird and me, to find some rhythm and by the time Mum and Dad arrived at William's house to fetch me, the little bird was gobbling food, raising its head eagerly towards the nib of the dropper. William told Mum and Dad what a great job I'd done and how I should come back tomorrow to feed the bird because I was so good at it. My parents weren't mad. They hugged me, then looked over my shoulder as I fed the baby bird some more. My dad shook hands with William and they talked in low voices until it was time to leave. My mum carried me to the car and we drove, Mum and Dad and me, all through the darkness until we were home.

Acknowledgements

FIRSTLY, THANKS TO EVERYONE at Picador for helping me to assemble and refine these stories into a coherent collection, especially Mathilda Imlah and Georgia Douglas. My thanks to Emma Schwarcz for her eagle eye and sensitive and sensible editing advice. My deep appreciation also to all those publishers, editors and proofreaders of the literary journals who published some of these pieces in the first place, and in many cases made them better with their excellent advice and great expertise. The talent, judgement and sheer enthusiasm of such people within the literary ecosystem should never be underestimated. Among them are: Louise Swinn, Zoe Dattner, Aviva Tuffield, Sophie Cunningham, Sally Breen, Rebecca Starford, Hannah Kent, Ian See, Jonathan Green, Ted Hodgkinson, Julianne Schultz, Matthew Lamb and Geordie Williamson. My sincere appreciation goes also to the Victorian Government through Creative Victoria for providing me with funding that allowed me to find time to complete a number of these stories. And, last but not least, thanks to Roslyn for all that gold and Reuben for all the cuddles. Couldn't have done it without you.

Details of previous publication

Headful of Bees first published in *The Sleepers Almanac X*, 2015

The Possibility of Water first published in *Griffith Review*, 2008

The Very Edge of Things first published in *Meanjin*, 2009

Growing Pain first published in *The Big Issue*, 2007

Petrichor first published in *Island*, 2017

The Middle of Nowhere first published in *Griffith Review*, 2011

The Other Side of Silence first published in *Griffith Review*, 2009

The Mare's Nest first published in *Review of Australian Fiction*, 2014

The Age of Terror first published in *Readings and Writings*, 2009

Where There's Smoke first published in *The Big Issue*, 2011

Season of Hope first published in *Griffith Review*, 2016

Chris Womersley

A Lovely and Terrible Thing first published in *Granta*, 2011
Blood Brother first published in *Meanjin*, 2017
The Shed first published in *Granta New Writing 14*, 2006
Theories of Relativity first published in *Kill Your Darlings*, 2010
What the Darkness Said first published in *Wet Ink*, 2008